WAR AND PEACE
BOOK TWO : 1805

By Leo Tolstoy

Double 9
BOOKS

War and Peace Book 2
by Leo Tolstoy

ISBN: 978-93-94973-33-6

Published by

DOUBLE 9 BOOKS

2/13-B, Ansari Road
Daryaganj, New Delhi - 110002
info@double9books.com
www.double9books.com
Tel. 011-40042856

Printed in India.

About the Author

L eo Tolstoy was a Russian creator known for his books War and Peace which is viewed as the best book of pragmatist fiction. Tolstoy is additionally viewed as world's best author by quite a few people. Additionally an ethical scholar and a social reformer, Tolstoy had extreme moralistic points of view. In later life, he turned into an intense Christian rebel and anarcho-conservative.

Leo Tolstoy Born in Yasnaya Polyana on September 9, 1828, He had a place with a notable honorable Russian family. He was the fourth among five offspring of Count Nikolai Ilyich Tolstoy and Countess Mariya Tolstaya, both of whom kicked the bucket passing on their youngsters to be raised by family members.

In 1844, Tolstoy was acknowledged into Kazan University. Incapable to graduate past the subsequent year, Tolstoy got back to Yasnava Polyana and afterward invested energy going among Moscow and St. Petersburg. With some functioning information on a few dialects, he turned into a multilingual. Yet again the recently observed youth pulled in Tolstoy towards drinking, visiting massage parlors and most betting which left him in weighty obligation and anguish however Tolstoy before long acknowledged he was carrying on with a brutish life and endeavored college tests with the expectation that he would acquire a situation with the public authority, yet finished yet up in Caucuses serving in the military continuing in the strides of his senior sibling.

In Year 1862, Leo Tolstoy wedded Sophia Andreevna Behrs, generally called Sonya, who was 16 years more youthful than him. The couple had thirteen youngsters, of which, five passed on at an early age. Sonya went about as Tolstoy's secretary, editor and monetary chief while he made two out of his most prominent works. Their initial wedded life was loaded up with happiness.

He started composing his show-stopper, War and Peace in 1862. The six volumes of the work were distributed somewhere in the range of 1863 and 1869. With 580 characters got from history and others made by Tolstoy, this extraordinary novel takes on investigating the hypothesis of history and the irrelevance of noted figures like Alexander and Napoleon. Anna Karenina, Tolstoy's next epic was begun in 1873 and distributed totally in 1878.

Contents

BOOK TWO : 1805

CHAPTER I

In October, 1805, a Russian army was occupying the villages and towns of the Archduchy of Austria, and yet other regiments freshly arriving from Russia were settling near the fortress of Braunau and burdening the inhabitants on whom they were quartered. Braunau was the headquarters of the commander in chief, Kutúzov.

On October 11, 1805, one of the infantry regiments that had just reached Braunau had halted half a mile from the town, waiting to be inspected by the commander in chief. Despite the un-Russian appearance of the locality and surroundings—fruit gardens, stone fences, tiled roofs, and hills in the distance—and despite the fact that the inhabitants (who gazed with curiosity at the soldiers) were not Russians, the regiment had just the appearance of any Russian regiment preparing for an inspection anywhere in the heart of Russia.

On the evening of the last day's march an order had been received that the commander in chief would inspect the regiment on the march. Though the words of the order were not clear to the regimental commander, and the question arose whether the troops were to be in marching order or not, it was decided at a consultation between the battalion commanders to present the regiment in parade order, on the principle that it is always better to "bow too low than not bow low enough." So the soldiers, after a twenty-mile march, were kept mending and cleaning all night long without closing their eyes, while the adjutants and company commanders calculated and reckoned, and by morning the regiment—instead of the straggling, disorderly crowd it had been on its last march the day before—presented a well-ordered array of two thousand men each of whom knew his place and his duty, had every button and every strap in place, and shone with cleanliness. And not only externally was all in order, but had it pleased the commander in chief to look under the uniforms he would have found on every man a clean shirt, and in every knapsack the appointed number of articles, "awl, soap, and all," as the soldiers say. There was only one circumstance concerning which no one could be at ease. It was the state of the soldiers' boots. More than half the men's boots were in holes. But this defect was not due to any fault of the regimental commander, for in spite of repeated demands boots had not been issued by the Austrian commissariat, and the regiment had marched some seven hundred miles.

The commander of the regiment was an elderly, choleric, stout, and thick-set general with grizzled eyebrows and whiskers, and wider from chest to back than across the shoulders. He had on a brand-new uniform showing the creases where it had been folded and thick gold epaulettes which seemed to stand rather than lie down on his massive shoulders. He had the air of a man happily performing one of the most solemn duties of his life. He walked about in front of the line and at every step pulled himself up, slightly arching his back. It was plain that the commander admired his regiment, rejoiced in it, and that his whole mind was engrossed by it, yet his strut seemed to indicate that, besides military matters, social interests and the fair sex occupied no small part of his thoughts.

"Well, Michael Mítrich, sir?" he said, addressing one of the battalion commanders who smilingly pressed forward (it was plain that they both felt happy). "We had our hands full last night. However, I think the regiment is not a bad one, eh?"

The battalion commander perceived the jovial irony and laughed.

"It would not be turned off the field even on the Tsarítsin Meadow."

"What?" asked the commander.

At that moment, on the road from the town on which signalers had been posted, two men appeared on horse back. They were an aide-de-camp followed by a Cossack.

The aide-de-camp was sent to confirm the order which had not been clearly worded the day before, namely, that the commander in chief wished to see the regiment just in the state in which it had been on the march: in their greatcoats, and packs, and without any preparation whatever.

A member of the Hofkriegsrath from Vienna had come to Kutúzov the day before with proposals and demands for him to join up with the army of the Archduke Ferdinand and Mack, and Kutúzov, not considering this junction advisable, meant, among other arguments in support of his view, to show the Austrian general the wretched state in which the troops arrived from Russia. With this object he intended to meet the regiment; so the worse the condition it was in, the better pleased the commander in chief would be. Though the aide-de-camp did not know these circumstances, he nevertheless delivered the definite order that the men should be in their greatcoats and in marching order, and that the commander in chief would otherwise be dissatisfied. On hearing this the regimental commander hung his head, silently shrugged his shoulders, and spread out his arms with a choleric gesture.

"A fine mess we've made of it!" he remarked.

"There now! Didn't I tell you, Michael Mítrich, that if it was said 'on the march' it meant in greatcoats?" said he reproachfully to the battalion commander. "Oh, my God!" he added, stepping resolutely forward. "Company commanders!" he shouted in a voice accustomed to command. "Sergeants major!... How soon will he be here?" he asked the aide-de-camp with a respectful politeness evidently relating to the personage he was referring to.

"In an hour's time, I should say."

"Shall we have time to change clothes?"

"I don't know, General...."

The regimental commander, going up to the line himself, ordered the soldiers to change into their greatcoats. The company commanders ran off to their companies, the sergeants major began bustling (the greatcoats were not in very good condition), and instantly the squares that had up to then been in regular order and silent began to sway and stretch and hum with voices. On all sides soldiers were running to and fro, throwing up their knapsacks with a jerk of their shoulders and pulling the straps over their heads, unstrapping their overcoats and drawing the sleeves on with upraised arms.

In half an hour all was again in order, only the squares had become gray instead of black. The regimental commander walked with his jerky steps to the front of the regiment and examined it from a distance.

"Whatever is this? This!" he shouted and stood still. "Commander of the third company!"

"Commander of the third company wanted by the general!... commander to the general... third company to the commander." The words passed along the lines and an adjutant ran to look for the missing officer.

When the eager but misrepeated words had reached their destination in a cry of: "The general to the third company," the missing officer appeared from behind his company and, though he was a middle-aged man and not in the habit of running, trotted awkwardly stumbling on his toes toward the general. The captain's face showed the uneasiness of a schoolboy who is told to repeat a lesson he has not learned. Spots appeared on his nose, the redness of which was evidently due to intemperance, and his mouth twitched nervously. The general looked the captain up and down as he came up panting, slackening his pace as he approached.

"You will soon be dressing your men in petticoats! What is this?" shouted the regimental commander, thrusting forward his jaw and pointing at a soldier in the ranks of the third company in a greatcoat of bluish cloth, which contrasted with the others. "What have you been after? The commander in chief is expected and you leave your place? Eh? I'll teach you to dress the men in fancy coats for a parade.... Eh...?"

The commander of the company, with his eyes fixed on his superior, pressed two fingers more and more rigidly to his cap, as if in this pressure lay his only hope of salvation.

"Well, why don't you speak? Whom have you got there dressed up as a Hungarian?" said the commander with an austere gibe.

"Your excellency..."

"Well, your excellency, what? Your excellency! But what about your excellency?... nobody knows."

"Your excellency, it's the officer Dólokhov, who has been reduced to the ranks," said the captain softly.

"Well? Has he been degraded into a field marshal, or into a soldier? If a soldier, he should be dressed in regulation uniform like the others."

"Your excellency, you gave him leave yourself, on the march."

"Gave him leave? Leave? That's just like you young men," said the regimental commander cooling down a little. "Leave indeed.... One says a word to you and you... What?" he added with renewed irritation, "I beg you to dress your men decently."

And the commander, turning to look at the adjutant, directed his jerky steps down the line. He was evidently pleased at his own display of anger and walking up to the regiment wished to find a further excuse for wrath. Having snapped at an officer for an unpolished badge, at another because his line was not straight, he reached the third company.

"H-o-o-w are you standing? Where's your leg? Your leg?" shouted the commander with a tone of suffering in his voice, while there were still five men between him and Dólokhov with his bluish-gray uniform.

Dólokhov slowly straightened his bent knee, looking straight with his clear, insolent eyes in the general's face.

"Why a blue coat? Off with it... Sergeant major! Change his coat... the ras..." he did not finish.

"General, I must obey orders, but I am not bound to endure..." Dólokhov hurriedly interrupted.

"No talking in the ranks!... No talking, no talking!"

"Not bound to endure insults," Dólokhov concluded in loud, ringing tones.

The eyes of the general and the soldier met. The general became silent, angrily pulling down his tight scarf.

"I request you to have the goodness to change your coat," he said as he turned away.

CHAPTER II

"He's coming!" shouted the signaler at that moment.

The regimental commander, flushing, ran to his horse, seized the stirrup with trembling hands, threw his body across the saddle, righted himself, drew his saber, and with a happy and resolute countenance, opening his mouth awry, prepared to shout. The regiment fluttered like a bird preening its plumage and became motionless.

"Att-ention!" shouted the regimental commander in a soul-shaking voice which expressed joy for himself, severity for the regiment, and welcome for the approaching chief.

Along the broad country road, edged on both sides by trees, came a high, light blue Viennese *calèche*, slightly creaking on its springs and drawn by six horses at a smart trot. Behind the *calèche* galloped the suite and a convoy of Croats. Beside Kutúzov sat an Austrian general, in a white uniform that looked strange among the Russian black ones. The *calèche* stopped in front of the regiment. Kutúzov and the Austrian general were talking in low voices and Kutúzov smiled slightly as treading heavily he stepped down from the carriage just as if those two thousand men breathlessly gazing at him and the regimental commander did not exist.

The word of command rang out, and again the regiment quivered, as with a jingling sound it presented arms. Then amidst a dead silence the feeble voice of the commander in chief was heard. The regiment roared, "Health to your ex... len... len... lency!" and again all became silent. At first Kutúzov stood still while the regiment moved; then he and the general in white, accompanied by the suite, walked between the ranks.

From the way the regimental commander saluted the commander in chief and devoured him with his eyes, drawing himself up obsequiously, and from the way he walked through the ranks behind the generals, bending forward and hardly able to restrain his jerky movements, and from the way he darted forward at every word or gesture of the commander in chief, it was evident that he performed his duty as a subordinate with even greater zeal than his duty as a commander. Thanks to the strictness and assiduity of its commander the regiment, in comparison with others that had reached Braunau at the same time, was in splendid condition. There were only 217 sick and stragglers. Everything was in good order except the boots.

Kutúzov walked through the ranks, sometimes stopping to say a few friendly words to officers he had known in the Turkish war, sometimes also to the soldiers. Looking at their boots he several times shook his head sadly, pointing them out to the Austrian general with an expression which seemed to say that he was not blaming anyone, but could not help noticing what a bad state of things it was. The regimental commander ran forward on each such occasion, fearing to miss a single word of the commander in chief's regarding the regiment. Behind Kutúzov, at a distance that allowed every softly spoken word to be heard, followed some twenty men of his suite. These gentlemen talked among themselves and sometimes laughed. Nearest of all to the commander in chief walked a handsome adjutant. This was Prince Bolkónski. Beside him was his comrade Nesvítski, a tall staff officer, extremely stout, with a kindly, smiling, handsome face and moist eyes. Nesvítski could hardly keep from laughter provoked by a swarthy hussar officer who walked beside him. This hussar, with a grave face and without a smile or a change in the expression of his fixed eyes, watched the regimental commander's back and mimicked his every movement. Each time the commander started and bent forward, the hussar started and bent forward in exactly the same manner. Nesvítski laughed and nudged the others to make them look at the wag.

Kutúzov walked slowly and languidly past thousands of eyes which were starting from their sockets to watch their chief. On reaching the third company he suddenly stopped. His suite, not having expected this, involuntarily came closer to him.

"Ah, Timókhin!" said he, recognizing the red-nosed captain who had been reprimanded on account of the blue greatcoat.

One would have thought it impossible for a man to stretch himself more than Timókhin had done when he was reprimanded by the regimental commander, but now that the commander in chief addressed him he drew himself up to such an extent that it seemed he could not have sustained it had the commander in chief continued to look at him, and so Kutúzov, who evidently understood his case and wished him nothing but good, quickly turned away, a scarcely perceptible smile flitting over his scarred and puffy face.

"Another Ismail comrade," said he. "A brave officer! Are you satisfied with him?" he asked the regimental commander.

And the latter—unconscious that he was being reflected in the hussar officer as in a looking glass—started, moved forward, and answered: "Highly satisfied, your excellency!"

"We all have our weaknesses," said Kutúzov smiling and walking away from him. "He used to have a predilection for Bacchus."

The regimental commander was afraid he might be blamed for this and did not answer. The hussar at that moment noticed the face of the red-nosed captain and his drawn-in stomach, and mimicked his expression and pose with such exactitude that Nesvítski could not help laughing. Kutúzov turned round. The officer evidently had complete control of his face, and while Kutúzov was turning managed to make a grimace and then assume a most serious, deferential, and innocent expression.

The third company was the last, and Kutúzov pondered, apparently trying to recollect something. Prince Andrew stepped forward from among the suite and said in French:

"You told me to remind you of the officer Dólokhov, reduced to the ranks in this regiment."

"Where is Dólokhov?" asked Kutúzov.

Dólokhov, who had already changed into a soldier's gray greatcoat, did not wait to be called. The shapely figure of the fair-haired soldier, with his clear blue eyes, stepped forward from the ranks, went up to the commander in chief, and presented arms.

"Have you a complaint to make?" Kutúzov asked with a slight frown.

"This is Dólokhov," said Prince Andrew.

"Ah!" said Kutúzov. "I hope this will be a lesson to you. Do your duty. The Emperor is gracious, and I shan't forget you if you deserve well."

The clear blue eyes looked at the commander in chief just as boldly as they had looked at the regimental commander, seeming by their expression to tear open the veil of convention that separates a commander in chief so widely from a private.

"One thing I ask of your excellency," Dólokhov said in his firm, ringing, deliberate voice. "I ask an opportunity to atone for my fault and prove my devotion to His Majesty the Emperor and to Russia!"

Kutúzov turned away. The same smile of the eyes with which he had turned from Captain Timókhin again flitted over his face. He turned away with a grimace as if to say that everything Dólokhov had said to him and everything he could say had long been known to him, that he was weary of it and it was not at all what he wanted. He turned away and went to the carriage.

The regiment broke up into companies, which went to their appointed quarters near Braunau, where they hoped to receive boots and clothes and to rest after their hard marches.

"You won't bear me a grudge, ProkhórIgnátych?" said the regimental commander, overtaking the third company on its way to its quarters and riding up to Captain Timókhin who was walking in front. (The regimental commander's face now that the inspection was happily over beamed with irrepressible delight.) "It's in the Emperor's service... it can't be helped... one is sometimes a bit hasty on parade... I am the first to apologize, you know me!... He was very pleased!" And he held out his hand to the captain.

"Don't mention it, General, as if I'd be so bold!" replied the captain, his nose growing redder as he gave a smile which showed where two front teeth were missing that had been knocked out by the butt end of a gun at Ismail.

"And tell Mr. Dólokhov that I won't forget him—he may be quite easy. And tell me, please—I've been meaning to ask—how is he behaving himself, and in general..."

"As far as the service goes he is quite punctilious, your excellency; but his character..." said Timókhin.

"And what about his character?" asked the regimental commander.

"It's different on different days," answered the captain. "One day he is sensible, well educated, and good-natured, and the next he's a wild beast.... In Poland, if you please, he nearly killed a Jew."

"Oh, well, well!" remarked the regimental commander. "Still, one must have pity on a young man in misfortune. You know he has important connections... Well, then, you just..."

"I will, your excellency," said Timókhin, showing by his smile that he understood his commander's wish.

"Well, of course, of course!"

The regimental commander sought out Dólokhov in the ranks and, reining in his horse, said to him:

"After the next affair... epaulettes."

Dólokhov looked round but did not say anything, nor did the mocking smile on his lips change.

"Well, that's all right," continued the regimental commander. "A cup of vodka for the men from me," he added so that the soldiers could hear. "I thank you all! God be praised!" and he rode past that company and overtook the next one.

"Well, he's really a good fellow, one can serve under him," said Timókhin to the subaltern beside him.

"In a word, a hearty one..." said the subaltern, laughing (the regimental commander was nicknamed *King of Hearts*).

The cheerful mood of their officers after the inspection infected the soldiers. The company marched on gaily. The soldiers' voices could be heard on every side.

"And they said Kutúzov was blind of one eye?"

"And so he is! Quite blind!"

"No, friend, he is sharper-eyed than you are. Boots and leg bands... he noticed everything..."

"When he looked at my feet, friend... well, thinks I..."

"And that other one with him, the Austrian, looked as if he were smeared with chalk—as white as flour! I suppose they polish him up as they do the guns."

"I say, Fédeshon!... Did he say when the battles are to begin? You were near him. Everybody said that Buonaparte himself was at Braunau."

"Buonaparte himself!... Just listen to the fool, what he doesn't know! The Prussians are up in arms now. The Austrians, you see, are putting them down. When they've been put down, the war with Buonaparte will begin. And he says Buonaparte is in Braunau! Shows you're a fool. You'd better listen more carefully!"

"What devils these quartermasters are! See, the fifth company is turning into the village already... they will have their buckwheat cooked before we reach our quarters."

"Give me a biscuit, you devil!"

"And did you give me tobacco yesterday? That's just it, friend! Ah, well, never mind, here you are."

"They might call a halt here or we'll have to do another four miles without eating."

"Wasn't it fine when those Germans gave us lifts! You just sit still and are drawn along."

"And here, friend, the people are quite beggarly. There they all seemed to be Poles—all under the Russian crown—but here they're all regular Germans."

"Singers to the front" came the captain's order.

And from the different ranks some twenty men ran to the front. A drummer, their leader, turned round facing the singers, and flourishing his arm, began a long-drawn-out soldiers' song, commencing with the words: *"Morning dawned, the sun was rising,"* and concluding: *"On then, brothers, on to glory, led by Father Kámenski."* This song had been composed in the Turkish campaign and now being sung in Austria, the only change being that the words "Father Kámenski" were replaced by "Father Kutúzov."

Having jerked out these last words as soldiers do and waved his arms as if flinging something to the ground, the drummer—a lean, handsome soldier of forty—looked sternly at the singers and screwed up his eyes. Then having satisfied himself that all eyes were fixed on him, he raised both arms as if carefully lifting some invisible but precious object above his head and, holding it there for some seconds, suddenly flung it down and began:

"Oh, my bower, oh, my bower...!"

"Oh, my bower new...!" chimed in twenty voices, and the castanet player, in spite of the burden of his equipment, rushed out to the front

and, walking backwards before the company, jerked his shoulders and flourished his castanets as if threatening someone. The soldiers, swinging their arms and keeping time spontaneously, marched with long steps. Behind the company the sound of wheels, the creaking of springs, and the tramp of horses' hoofs were heard. Kutúzov and his suite were returning to the town. The commander in chief made a sign that the men should continue to march at ease, and he and all his suite showed pleasure at the sound of the singing and the sight of the dancing soldier and the gay and smartly marching men. In the second file from the right flank, beside which the carriage passed the company, a blue-eyed soldier involuntarily attracted notice. It was Dólokhov marching with particular grace and boldness in time to the song and looking at those driving past as if he pitied all who were not at that moment marching with the company. The hussar cornet of Kutúzov's suite who had mimicked the regimental commander, fell back from the carriage and rode up to Dólokhov.

Hussar cornet Zherkóv had at one time, in Petersburg, belonged to the wild set led by Dólokhov. Zherkóv had met Dólokhov abroad as a private and had not seen fit to recognize him. But now that Kutúzov had spoken to the gentleman ranker, he addressed him with the cordiality of an old friend.

"My dear fellow, how are you?" said he through the singing, making his horse keep pace with the company.

"How am I?" Dólokhov answered coldly. "I am as you see."

The lively song gave a special flavor to the tone of free and easy gaiety with which Zherkóv spoke, and to the intentional coldness of Dólokhov's reply.

"And how do you get on with the officers?" inquired Zherkóv.

"All right. They are good fellows. And how have you wriggled onto the staff?"

"I was attached; I'm on duty."

Both were silent.

"She let the hawk fly upward from her wide right sleeve," went the song, arousing an involuntary sensation of courage and cheerfulness. Their conversation would probably have been different but for the effect of that song.

"Is it true that Austrians have been beaten?" asked Dólokhov.

"The devil only knows! They say so."

"I'm glad," answered Dólokhov briefly and clearly, as the song demanded.

"I say, come round some evening and we'll have a game of faro!" said Zherkóv.

"Why, have you too much money?"

"Do come."

"I can't. I've sworn not to. I won't drink and won't play till I get reinstated."

"Well, that's only till the first engagement."

"We shall see."

They were again silent.

"Come if you need anything. One can at least be of use on the staff..."

Dólokhov smiled. "Don't trouble. If I want anything, I won't beg—I'll take it!"

"Well, never mind; I only..."

"And I only..."

"Good-by."

"Good health..."

"It's a long, long way. To my native land..."

Zherkóv touched his horse with the spurs; it pranced excitedly from foot to foot uncertain with which to start, then settled down, galloped past the company, and overtook the carriage, still keeping time to the song.

CHAPTER III

On returning from the review, Kutúzov took the Austrian general into his private room and, calling his adjutant, asked for some papers relating to the condition of the troops on their arrival, and the letters that had come from the Archduke Ferdinand, who was in command of the advanced army. Prince Andrew Bolkónski came into the room with the required papers. Kutúzov and the Austrian member of the Hofkriegsrath were sitting at the table on which a plan was spread out.

"Ah!..." said Kutúzov glancing at Bolkónski as if by this exclamation he was asking the adjutant to wait, and he went on with the conversation in French.

"All I can say, General," said he with a pleasant elegance of expression and intonation that obliged one to listen to each deliberately spoken word. It was evident that Kutúzov himself listened with pleasure to his own voice. "All I can say, General, is that if the matter depended on my personal wishes, the will of His Majesty the Emperor Francis would have been fulfilled long ago. I should long ago have joined the archduke. And believe me on my honour that to me personally it would be a pleasure to hand over the supreme command of the army into the hands of a better informed and more skillful general—of whom Austria has so many—and to lay down all this heavy responsibility. But circumstances are sometimes too strong for us, General."

And Kutúzov smiled in a way that seemed to say, "You are quite at liberty not to believe me and I don't even care whether you do or not, but you have no grounds for telling me so. And that is the whole point."

The Austrian general looked dissatisfied, but had no option but to reply in the same tone.

"On the contrary," he said, in a querulous and angry tone that contrasted with his flattering words, "on the contrary, your excellency's participation in the common action is highly valued by His Majesty; but we think the present delay is depriving the splendid Russian troops and their commander of the laurels they have been accustomed to win in their battles," he concluded his evidently prearranged sentence.

Kutúzov bowed with the same smile.

"But that is my conviction, and judging by the last letter with which His Highness the Archduke Ferdinand has honored me, I imagine that the Austrian troops, under the direction of so skillful a leader as General Mack, have by now already gained a decisive victory and no longer need our aid," said Kutúzov.

The general frowned. Though there was no definite news of an Austrian defeat, there were many circumstances confirming the unfavorablerumors that were afloat, and so Kutúzov's suggestion of an Austrian victory sounded much like irony. But Kutúzov went on blandly smiling with the same expression, which seemed to say that he had a right to suppose so. And, in fact, the last letter he had received from Mack's army informed him of a victory and stated strategically the position of the army was very favorable.

"Give me that letter," said Kutúzov turning to Prince Andrew. "Please have a look at it"—and Kutúzov with an ironical smile about the corners of his mouth read to the Austrian general the following passage, in German, from the Archduke Ferdinand's letter:

We have fully concentrated forces of nearly seventy thousand men with which to attack and defeat the enemy should he cross the Lech. Also, as we are masters of Ulm, we cannot be deprived of the advantage of commanding both sides of the Danube, so that should the enemy not cross the Lech, we can cross the Danube, throw ourselves on his line of communications, recross the river lower down, and frustrate his intention should he try to direct his whole force against our faithful ally. We shall therefore confidently await the moment when the Imperial Russian army will be fully equipped, and shall then, in conjunction with it, easily find a way to prepare for the enemy the fate he deserves.

Kutúzov sighed deeply on finishing this paragraph and looked at the member of the Hofkriegsrath mildly and attentively.

"But you know the wise maxim your excellency, advising one to expect the worst," said the Austrian general, evidently wishing to have done with jests and to come to business. He involuntarily looked round at the aide-de-camp.

"Excuse me, General," interrupted Kutúzov, also turning to Prince Andrew. "Look here, my dear fellow, get from Kozlóvski all the reports from our scouts. Here are two letters from Count Nostitz and here is one from His Highness the Archduke Ferdinand and here are these," he said, handing him several papers, "make a neat memorandum in French out of all this, showing all the news we have had of the movements of the Austrian army, and then give it to his excellency."

Prince Andrew bowed his head in token of having understood from the first not only what had been said but also what Kutúzov would have liked to tell him. He gathered up the papers and with a bow to both, stepped softly over the carpet and went out into the waiting room.

Though not much time had passed since Prince Andrew had left Russia, he had changed greatly during that period. In the expression of his face, in his movements, in his walk, scarcely a trace was left of his former affected languor and indolence. He now looked like a man who has time to think of the impression he makes on others, but is occupied with agreeable and interesting work. His face expressed more satisfaction with himself and those around him, his smile and glance were brighter and more attractive.

Kutúzov, whom he had overtaken in Poland, had received him very kindly, promised not to forget him, distinguished him above the other adjutants, and had taken him to Vienna and given him the more serious commissions. From Vienna Kutúzov wrote to his old comrade, Prince Andrew's father.

Your son bids fair to become an officer distinguished by his industry, firmness, and expedition. I consider myself fortunate to have such a subordinate by me.

On Kutúzov's staff, among his fellow officers and in the army generally, Prince Andrew had, as he had had in Petersburg society, two quite opposite reputations. Some, a minority, acknowledged him to be different from themselves and from everyone else, expected great things of him, listened to him, admired, and imitated him, and with them Prince Andrew was natural and pleasant. Others, the majority, disliked him and considered him conceited, cold, and disagreeable. But among these people Prince Andrew knew how to take his stand so that they respected and even feared him.

Coming out of Kutúzov's room into the waiting room with the papers in his hand Prince Andrew came up to his comrade, the aide-de-camp on duty, Kozlóvski, who was sitting at the window with a book.

"Well, Prince?" asked Kozlóvski.

"I am ordered to write a memorandum explaining why we are not advancing."

"And why is it?"

Prince Andrew shrugged his shoulders.

"Any news from Mack?"

"No."

"If it were true that he has been beaten, news would have come."

"Probably," said Prince Andrew moving toward the outer door.

But at that instant a tall Austrian general in a greatcoat, with the order of Maria Theresa on his neck and a black bandage round his head, who had evidently just arrived, entered quickly, slamming the door. Prince Andrew stopped short.

"Commander in Chief Kutúzov?" said the newly arrived general speaking quickly with a harsh German accent, looking to both sides and advancing straight toward the inner door.

"The commander in chief is engaged," said Kozlóvski, going hurriedly up to the unknown general and blocking his way to the door. "Whom shall I announce?"

The unknown general looked disdainfully down at Kozlóvski, who was rather short, as if surprised that anyone should not know him.

"The commander in chief is engaged," repeated Kozlóvski calmly.

The general's face clouded, his lips quivered and trembled. He took out a notebook, hurriedly scribbled something in pencil, tore out the leaf, gave it to Kozlóvski, stepped quickly to the window, and threw himself into a chair, gazing at those in the room as if asking, "Why do they look at me?" Then he lifted his head, stretched his neck as if he intended to say something, but immediately, with affected indifference, began to hum to himself, producing a queer sound which immediately broke off. The door of the private room opened and Kutúzov appeared in the doorway. The general with the bandaged head bent forward as though running away from some danger, and, making long, quick strides with his thin legs, went up to Kutúzov.

"Vousvoyez le malheureux Mack," he uttered in a broken voice.

Kutúzov's face as he stood in the open doorway remained perfectly immobile for a few moments. Then wrinkles ran over his face like a wave and his forehead became smooth again, he bowed his head respectfully, closed his eyes, silently let Mack enter his room before him, and closed the door himself behind him.

The report which had been circulated that the Austrians had been beaten and that the whole army had surrendered at Ulm proved to be correct. Within half an hour adjutants had been sent in various directions with orders which showed that the Russian troops, who had hitherto been inactive, would also soon have to meet the enemy.

Prince Andrew was one of those rare staff officers whose chief interest lay in the general progress of the war. When he saw Mack and heard the details of his disaster he understood that half the campaign was lost, understood all the difficulties of the Russian army's position, and vividly imagined what awaited it and the part he would have to play. Involuntarily he felt a joyful agitation at the thought of the humiliation of arrogant Austria and that in a week's time he might, perhaps, see and take part in the first Russian encounter with the French since Suvórov met them. He feared that Bonaparte's genius might outweigh all the courage of the Russian troops, and at the same time could not admit the idea of his hero being disgraced.

Excited and irritated by these thoughts Prince Andrew went toward his room to write to his father, to whom he wrote every day. In the corridor he met Nesvítski, with whom he shared a room, and the wag Zherkóv; they were as usual laughing.

"Why are you so glum?" asked Nesvítski noticing Prince Andrew's pale face and glittering eyes.

"There's nothing to be gay about," answered Bolkónski.

Just as Prince Andrew metJust as Prince Andrew met Nesvítski and Zherkóv, there came toward them from the other end of the corridor, Strauch, an Austrian general who was on Kutúzov's staff in charge of the provisioning of the Russian army, and the member of the Hofkriegsrath who had arrived the previous evening. There was room enough in the wide corridor for the generals to pass the three officers quite easily, but Zherkóv, pushing Nesvítski aside with his arm, said in a breathless voice,

"They're coming!... they're coming!... Stand aside, make way, please make way!"

The generals were passing by, looking as if they wished to avoid embarrassing attentions. On the face of the wag Zherkóv there suddenly appeared a stupid smile of glee which he seemed unable to suppress.

"Your excellency," said he in German, stepping forward and addressing the Austrian general, "I have the honor to congratulate you."

He bowed his head and scraped first with one foot and then with the other, awkwardly, like a child at a dancing lesson.

The member of the Hofkriegsrath looked at him severely but, seeing the seriousness of his stupid smile, could not but give him a moment's attention. He screwed up his eyes showing that he was listening.

"I have the honor to congratulate you. General Mack has arrived, quite well, only a little bruised just here," he added, pointing with a beaming smile to his head.

The general frowned, turned away, and went on.

"*Gott, wienaiv!*"* said he angrily, after he had gone a few steps.

* "Good God, what simplicity!"

Nesvítski with a laugh threw his arms round Prince Andrew, but Bolkónski, turning still paler, pushed him away with an angry look and turned to Zherkóv. The nervous irritation aroused by the appearance of Mack, the news of his defeat, and the thought of what lay before the Russian army found vent in anger at Zherkóv's untimely jest.

"If you, sir, choose to make a *buffoon* of yourself," he said sharply, with a slight trembling of the lower jaw, "I can't prevent your doing so; but I warn you that if you *dare* to play the fool in my presence, I will teach you to behave yourself."

Nesvítski and Zherkóv were so surprised by this outburst that they gazed at Bolkónski silently with wide-open eyes.

"What's the matter? I only congratulated them," said Zherkóv.

"I am not jesting with you; please be silent!" cried Bolkónski, and taking Nesvítski's arm he left Zherkóv, who did not know what to say.

"Come, what's the matter, old fellow?" said Nesvítski trying to soothe him.

"What's the matter?" exclaimed Prince Andrew standing still in his excitement. "Don't you understand that either we are officers serving our Tsar and our country, rejoicing in the successes and grieving at the misfortunes of our common cause, or we are merely lackeys who care nothing for their master's business. *Quarantemille hommes massacrés et l'armée de nosalliésdétruite, et voustrouvezlà le mot pourrire,"* * he said, as if strengthening his views by this French sentence. *"C'est bien pour un garçon de riencommecetindividudontvousavez fait un ami, mais pas pour vous, pas pour vous.* *(2) Only a *hobbledehoy* could amuse himself in this way," he added in Russian—but pronouncing the word with a French accent—having noticed that Zherkóv could still hear him.

* "Forty thousand men massacred and the army of our allies destroyed, and you find that a cause for jesting!"

* (2) "It is all very well for that good-for-nothing fellow of whom you have made a friend, but not for you, not for you."

He waited a moment to see whether the cornet would answer, but he turned and went out of the corridor.

CHAPTER IV

The Pávlograd Hussars were stationed two miles from Braunau. The squadron in which Nicholas Rostóv served as a cadet was quartered in the German village of Salzeneck. The best quarters in the village were assigned to cavalry-captain Denísov, the squadron commander, known throughout the whole cavalry division as VáskaDenísov. Cadet Rostóv, ever since he had overtaken the regiment in Poland, had lived with the squadron commander.

On October 11, the day when all was astir at headquarters over the news of Mack's defeat, the camp life of the officers of this squadron was proceeding as usual. Denísov, who had been losing at cards all night, had not yet come home when Rostóv rode back early in the morning from a foraging expedition. Rostóv in his cadet uniform, with a jerk to his horse, rode up to the porch, swung his leg over the saddle with a supple youthful movement, stood for a moment in the stirrup as if loathe to part from his horse, and at last sprang down and called to his orderly.

"Ah, Bondarénko, dear friend!" said he to the hussar who rushed up headlong to the horse. "Walk him up and down, my dear fellow," he continued, with that gay brotherly cordiality which goodhearted young people show to everyone when they are happy.

"Yes, your excellency," answered the Ukrainian gaily, tossing his head.

"Mind, walk him up and down well!"

Another hussar also rushed toward the horse, but Bondarénko had already thrown the reins of the snaffle bridle over the horse's head. It was evident that the cadet was liberal with his tips and that it paid to serve him. Rostóv patted the horse's neck and then his flank, and lingered for a moment.

"Splendid! What a horse he will be!" he thought with a smile, and holding up his saber, his spurs jingling, he ran up the steps of the porch. His landlord, who in a waistcoat and a pointed cap, pitchfork in hand, was clearing manure from the cowhouse, looked out, and his face immediately brightened on seeing Rostóv. "*Schön gut Morgen! Schön gut Morgen!*" * he said winking with a merry smile, evidently pleased to greet the young man.

* "A very good morning! A very good morning!"

"*Schon fleissig?*" * saidRostóv with the same gay brotherly smile which did not leave his eager face. "*Hoch Oestreicher! Hoch Russen! Kaiser Alexander hoch!*" *(2) said he, quoting words often repeated by the German landlord.

* "Busy already?"

* (2) "Hurrah for the Austrians! Hurrah for the Russians! Hurrah for Emperor Alexander!"

The German laughed, came out of the cowshed, pulled off his cap, and waving it above his head cried:

"*Und die ganze Welt hoch!*" *

* "And hurrah for the whole world!"

Rostóv waved his cap above his head like the German and cried laughing, "*Und vivat die ganze Welt!*" Though neither the German cleaning his cowshed nor Rostóv back with his platoon from foraging for hay had any reason for rejoicing, they looked at each other with joyful delight and brotherly love, wagged their heads in token of their mutual affection, and parted smiling, the German returning to his cowshed and Rostóv going to the cottage he occupied with Denísov.

"What about your master?" he asked Lavrúshka, Denísov's orderly, whom all the regiment knew for a rogue.

"Hasn't been in since the evening. Must have been losing," answered Lavrúshka. "I know by now, if he wins he comes back early to brag about it, but if he stays out till morning it means he's lost and will come back in a rage. Will you have coffee?"

"Yes, bring some."

Ten minutes later Lavrúshka brought the coffee. "He's coming!" said he. "Now for trouble!" Rostóv looked out of the window and saw Denísov coming home. Denísov was a small man with a red face, sparkling black eyes, and black tousled mustache and hair. He wore an unfastened cloak, wide breeches hanging down in creases, and a crumpled shako on the back of his head. He came up to the porch gloomily, hanging his head.

"Lavwúska!" he shouted loudly and angrily, "take it off, blockhead!"

"Well, I am taking it off," replied Lavrúshka's voice.

"Ah, you're up already," said Denísov, entering the room.

"Long ago," answered Rostóv, "I have already been for the hay, and have seen Fräulein Mathilde."

"Weally! And I've been losing, bwother. I lost yesterday like a damned fool!" cried Denísov, not pronouncing his r's. "Such ill luck! Such ill luck. As soon as you left, it began and went on. Hullo there! Tea!"

Puckering up his face though smiling, and showing his short strong teeth, he began with stubby fingers of both hands to ruffle up his thick tangled black hair.

"And what devil made me go to that wat?" (an officer nicknamed "the rat") he said, rubbing his forehead and whole face with both hands. "Just fancy, he didn't let me win a single cahd, not one cahd."

He took the lighted pipe that was offered to him, gripped it in his fist, and tapped it on the floor, making the sparks fly, while he continued to shout.

"He lets one win the singles and collahs it as soon as one doubles it; gives the singles and snatches the doubles!"

He scattered the burning tobacco, smashed the pipe, and threw it away. Then he remained silent for a while, and all at once looked cheerfully with his glittering, black eyes at Rostóv.

"If at least we had some women here; but there's nothing foh one to do but dwink. If we could only get to fighting soon. Hullo, who's there?" he said, turning to the door as he heard a tread of heavy boots and the clinking of spurs that came to a stop, and a respectful cough.

"The squadron quartermaster!" said Lavrúshka.

Denísov's face puckered still more.

"Wetched!" he muttered, throwing down a purse with some gold in it. "Wostóv, deah fellow, just see how much there is left and shove the purse undah the pillow," he said, and went out to the quartermaster.

Rostóv took the money and, mechanically arranging the old and new coins in separate piles, began counting them.

"Ah! Telyánin! How d'ye do? They plucked me last night," came Denísov's voice from the next room.

"Where? At Bykov's, at the rat's... I knew it," replied a piping voice, and Lieutenant Telyánin, a small officer of the same squadron, entered the room.

Rostóv thrust the purse under the pillow and shook the damp little hand which was offered him. Telyánin for some reason had been transferred from the Guards just before this campaign. He behaved very well in the regiment but was not liked; Rostóv especially detested him and was unable to overcome or conceal his groundless antipathy to the man.

"Well, young cavalryman, how is my Rook behaving?" he asked. (Rook was a young horse Telyánin had sold to Rostóv.)

The lieutenant never looked the man he was speaking to straight in the face; his eyes continually wandered from one object to another.

"I saw you riding this morning..." he added.

"Oh, he's all right, a good horse," answered Rostóv, though the horse for which he had paid seven hundred rubles was not worth half that sum. "He's begun to go a little lame on the left foreleg," he added.

"The hoof's cracked! That's nothing. I'll teach you what to do and show you what kind of rivet to use."

"Yes, please do," said Rostóv.

"I'll show you, I'll show you! It's not a secret. And it's a horse you'll thank me for."

"Then I'll have it brought round," said Rostóv wishing to avoid Telyánin, and he went out to give the order.

In the passage Denísov, with a pipe, was squatting on the threshold facing the quartermaster who was reporting to him. On seeing Rostóv, Denísov screwed up his face and pointing over his shoulder with his thumb to the room where Telyánin was sitting, he frowned and gave a shudder of disgust.

"Ugh! I don't like that fellow," he said, regardless of the quartermaster's presence.

Rostóv shrugged his shoulders as much as to say: "Nor do I, but what's one to do?" and, having given his order, he returned to Telyánin.

Telyánin was sitting in the same indolent pose in which Rostóv had left him, rubbing his small white hands.

"Well there certainly are disgusting people," thought Rostóv as he entered.

"Have you told them to bring the horse?" asked Telyánin, getting up and looking carelessly about him.

"I have."

"Let us go ourselves. I only came round to ask Denísov about yesterday's order. Have you got it, Denísov?"

"Not yet. But where are you off to?"

"I want to teach this young man how to shoe a horse," said Telyánin.

They went through the porch and into the stable. The lieutenant explained how to rivet the hoof and went away to his own quarters.

When Rostóv went back there was a bottle of vodka and a sausage on the table. Denísov was sitting there scratching with his pen on a sheet of paper. He looked gloomily in Rostóv's face and said: "I am witing to her."

He leaned his elbows on the table with his pen in his hand and, evidently glad of a chance to say quicker in words what he wanted to write, told Rostóv the contents of his letter.

"You see, my fwiend," he said, "we sleep when we don't love. We are childwen of the dust... but one falls in love and one is a God, one is pua' as on the fihst day of cweation... Who's that now? Send him to the devil, I'm busy!" he shouted to Lavrúshka, who went up to him not in the least abashed.

"Who should it be? You yourself told him to come. It's the quartermaster for the money."

Denísov frowned and was about to shout some reply but stopped.

"Wetched business," he muttered to himself. "How much is left in the puhse?" he asked, turning to Rostóv.

"Seven new and three old imperials."

"Oh, it's wetched! Well, what are you standing there for, you sca'cwow? Call the quahtehmasteh," he shouted to Lavrúshka.

"Please, Denísov, let me lend you some: I have some, you know," said Rostóv, blushing.

"Don't like bowwowing from my own fellows, I don't," growled Denísov.

"But if you won't accept money from me like a comrade, you will offend me. Really I have some," Rostóv repeated.

"No, I tell you."

And Denísov went to the bed to get the purse from under the pillow.

"Where have you put it, Wostóv?"

"Under the lower pillow."

"It's not there."

Denísov threw both pillows on the floor. The purse was not there.

"That's a miwacle."

"Wait, haven't you dropped it?" said Rostóv, picking up the pillows one at a time and shaking them.

He pulled off the quilt and shook it. The purse was not there.

"Dear me, can I have forgotten? No, I remember thinking that you kept it under your head like a treasure," said Rostóv. "I put it just here. Where is it?" he asked, turning to Lavrúshka.

"I haven't been in the room. It must be where you put it."

"But it isn't?..."

"You're always like that; you thwow a thing down anywhere and forget it. Feel in your pockets."

"No, if I hadn't thought of it being a treasure," said Rostóv, "but I remember putting it there."

Lavrúshka turned all the bedding over, looked under the bed and under the table, searched everywhere, and stood still in the middle of the room. Denísov silently watched Lavrúshka's movements, and when the latter threw up his arms in surprise saying it was nowhere to be found Denísov glanced at Rostóv.

"Wostóv, you've not been playing schoolboy twicks..."

Rostóv felt Denísov's gaze fixed on him, raised his eyes, and instantly dropped them again. All the blood which had seemed congested somewhere below his throat rushed to his face and eyes. He could not draw breath.

"And there hasn't been anyone in the room except the lieutenant and yourselves. It must be here somewhere," said Lavrúshka.

"Now then, you devil's puppet, look alive and hunt for it!" shouted Denísov, suddenly, turning purple and rushing at the man with a threatening gesture. "If the purse isn't found I'll flog you, I'll flog you all."

Rostóv, his eyes avoiding Denísov, began buttoning his coat, buckled on his saber, and put on his cap.

"I must have that purse, I tell you," shoutedDenísov, shaking his orderly by the shoulders and knocking him against the wall.

"Denísov, let him alone, I know who has taken it," said Rostóv, going toward the door without raising his eyes. Denísov paused, thought a moment, and, evidently understanding what Rostóv hinted at, seized his arm.

"Nonsense!" he cried, and the veins on his forehead and neck stood out like cords. "You are mad, I tell you. I won't allow it. The purse is here! I'll flay this scoundwel alive, and it will be found."

"I know who has taken it," repeated Rostóv in an unsteady voice, and went to the door.

"And I tell you, don't you dahe to do it!" shouted Denísov, rushing at the cadet to restrain him.

But Rostóv pulled away his arm and, with as much anger as though Denísov were his worst enemy, firmly fixed his eyes directly on his face.

"Do you understand what you're saying?" he said in a trembling voice. "There was no one else in the room except myself. So that if it is not so, then..."

He could not finish, and ran out of the room.

"Ah, may the devil take you and evewybody," were the last words Rostóv heard.

Rostóv went to Telyánin's quarters.

"The master is not in, he's gone to headquarters," said Telyánin's orderly. "Has something happened?" he added, surprised at the cadet's troubled face.

"No, nothing."

"You've only just missed him," said the orderly.

The headquarters were situated two miles away from Salzeneck, and Rostóv, without returning home, took a horse and rode there. There was an inn in the village which the officers frequented. Rostóv rode up to it and saw Telyánin's horse at the porch.

In the second room of the inn the lieutenant was sitting over a dish of sausages and a bottle of wine.

"Ah, you've come here too, young man!" he said, smiling and raising his eyebrows.

"Yes," said Rostóv as if it cost him a great deal to utter the word; and he sat down at the nearest table.

Both were silent. There were two Germans and a Russian officer in the room. No one spoke and the only sounds heard were the clatter of knives and the munching of the lieutenant.

When Telyánin had finished his lunch he took out of his pocket a double purse and, drawing its rings aside with his small, white, turned-up fingers, drew out a gold imperial, and lifting his eyebrows gave it to the waiter.

"Please be quick," he said.

The coin was a new one. Rostóv rose and went up to Telyánin.

"Allow me to look at your purse," he said in a low, almost inaudible, voice.

With shifting eyes but eyebrows still raised, Telyánin handed him the purse.

"Yes, it's a nice purse. Yes, yes," he said, growing suddenly pale, and added, "Look at it, young man."

Rostóv took the purse in his hand, examined it and the money in it, and looked at Telyánin. The lieutenant was looking about in his usual way and suddenly seemed to grow very merry.

"If we get to Vienna I'll get rid of it there but in these wretched little towns there's nowhere to spend it," said he. "Well, let me have it, young man, I'm going."

Rostóv did not speak.

"And you? Are you going to have lunch too? They feed you quite decently here," continued Telyánin. "Now then, let me have it."

He stretched out his hand to take hold of the purse. Rostóv let go of it. Telyánin took the purse and began carelessly slipping it into the pocket of his riding breeches, with his eyebrows lifted and his mouth slightly open, as if to say, "Yes, yes, I am putting my purse in my pocket and that's quite simple and is no one else's business."

"Well, young man?" he said with a sigh, and from under his lifted brows he glanced into Rostóv's eyes.

Some flash as of an electric spark shot from Telyánin's eyes to Rostóv's and back, and back again and again in an instant.

"Come here," said Rostóv, catching hold of Telyánin's arm and almost dragging him to the window. "That money is Denísov's; you took it..." he whispered just above Telyánin's ear.

"What? What? How dare you? What?" said Telyánin.

But these words came like a piteous, despairing cry and an entreaty for pardon. As soon as Rostóv heard them, an enormous load of doubt fell from him. He was glad, and at the same instant began to pity the miserable man who stood before him, but the task he had begun had to be completed.

"Heaven only knows what the people here may imagine," muttered Telyánin, taking up his cap and moving toward a small empty room. "We must have an explanation..."

"I know it and shall prove it," said Rostóv.

"I..."

Every muscle of Telyánin's pale, terrified face began to quiver, his eyes still shifted from side to side but with a downward look not rising to Rostóv's face, and his sobs were audible.

"Count!... Don't ruin a young fellow... here is this wretched money, take it..." He threw it on the table. "I have an old father and mother!..."

Rostóv took the money, avoiding Telyánin's eyes, and went out of the room without a word. But at the door he stopped and then retraced his steps. "O God," he said with tears in his eyes, "how could you do it?"

"Count..." said Telyánin drawing nearer to him.

"Don't touch me," said Rostóv, drawing back. "If you need it, take the money," and he threw the purse to him and ran out of the inn.

CHAPTER V

That same evening there was an animated discussion among the squadron's officers in Denísov's quarters.

"And I tell you, Rostóv, that you must apologize to the colonel!" said a tall, grizzly-haired staff captain, with enormous mustaches and many wrinkles on his large features, to Rostóv who was crimson with excitement.

The staff captain, Kírsten, had twice been reduced to the ranks for affairs of honor and had twice regained his commission.

"I will allow no one to call me a liar!" cried Rostóv. "He told me I lied, and I told him he lied. And there it rests. He may keep me on duty every day, or may place me under arrest, but no one can make me apologize, because if he, as commander of this regiment, thinks it beneath his dignity to give me satisfaction, then..."

"You just wait a moment, my dear fellow, and listen," interrupted the staff captain in his deep bass, calmly stroking his long mustache. "You tell the colonel in the presence of other officers that an officer has stolen..."

"I'm not to blame that the conversation began in the presence of other officers. Perhaps I ought not to have spoken before them, but I am not a diplomatist. That's why I joined the hussars, thinking that here one would not need finesse; and he tells me that I am lying—so let him give me satisfaction..."

"That's all right. No one thinks you a coward, but that's not the point. Ask Denísov whether it is not out of the question for a cadet to demand satisfaction of his regimental commander?"

Denísov sat gloomily biting his mustache and listening to the conversation, evidently with no wish to take part in it. He answered the staff captain's question by a disapproving shake of his head.

"You speak to the colonel about this nasty business before other officers," continued the staff captain, "and Bogdánich" (the colonel was called Bogdánich) "shuts you up."

"He did not shut me up, he said I was telling an untruth."

"Well, have it so, and you talked a lot of nonsense to him and must apologize."

"Not on any account!" exclaimed Rostóv.

"I did not expect this of you," said the staff captain seriously and severely. "You don't wish to apologize, but, man, it's not only to him but to the whole regiment—all of us—you're to blame all round. The case is this: you ought to have thought the matter over and taken advice; but no, you go and blurt it all straight out before the officers. Now what was the colonel to do? Have the officer tried and disgrace the whole regiment? Disgrace the whole regiment because of one scoundrel? Is that how you look at it? We don't see it like that. And Bogdánich was a brick: he told you you were saying what was not true. It's not pleasant, but what's to be done, my dear fellow? You landed yourself in it. And now, when one wants to smooth the thing over, some conceit prevents your apologizing, and you wish to make the whole affair public. You are offended at being put on duty a bit, but why not apologize to an old and honorable officer? Whatever Bogdánich may be, anyway he is an honorable and brave old colonel! You're quick at taking offense, but you don't mind disgracing the whole regiment!" The staff captain's voice began to tremble. "You have been in the regiment next to no time, my lad, you're here today and tomorrow you'll be appointed adjutant somewhere and can snap your fingers when it is said 'There are thieves among the Pávlograd officers!' But it's not all the same to us! Am I not right, Denísov? It's not the same!"

Denísov remained silent and did not move, but occasionally looked with his glittering black eyes at Rostóv.

"You value your own pride and don't wish to apologize," continued the staff captain, "but we old fellows, who have grown up in and, God willing, are going to die in the regiment, we prize the honor of the regiment, and Bogdánich knows it. Oh, we do prize it, old fellow! And all this is not right, it's not right! You may take offense or not but I always stick to mother truth. It's not right!"

And the staff captain rose and turned away from Rostóv.

"That's twue, devil take it!" shouted Denísov, jumping up. "Now then, Wostóv, now then!"

Rostóv, growing red and pale alternately, looked first at one officer and then at the other.

"No, gentlemen, no... you mustn't think... I quite understand. You're wrong to think that of me... I... for me... for the honor of the regiment I'd... Ah well, I'll show that in action, and for me the honor of the flag... Well, never mind, it's true I'm to blame, to blame all round. Well, what else do you want?..."

"Come, that's right, Count!" cried the staff captain, turning round and clapping Rostóv on the shoulder with his big hand.

" I tell you," shoutedDenísov, "he's a fine fellow."

"That's better, Count," said the staff captain, beginning to address Rostóv by his title, as if in recognition of his confession. "Go and apologize, your excellency. Yes, go!"

"Gentlemen, I'll do anything. No one shall hear a word from me," said Rostóv in an imploring voice, "but I can't apologize, by God I can't, do what you will! How can I go and apologize like a little boy asking forgiveness?"

Denísov began to laugh.

"It'll be worse for you. Bogdánich is vindictive and you'll pay for your obstinacy," said Kírsten.

"No, on my word it's not obstinacy! I can't describe the feeling. I can't..."

"Well, it's as you like," said the staff captain. "And what has become of that scoundrel?" he asked Denísov.

"He has weported himself sick, he's to be stwuck off the list tomowwow," muttered Denísov.

"It is an illness, there's no other way of explaining it," said the staff captain.

"Illness or not, he'd better not cwoss my path. I'd kill him!" shouted Denísov in a bloodthirsty tone.

Just then Zherkóv entered the room.

"What brings you here?" cried the officers turning to the newcomer.

"We're to go into action, gentlemen! Mack has surrendered with his whole army."

"It's not true!"

"I've seen him myself!"

"What? Saw the real Mack? With hands and feet?"

"Into action! Into action! Bring him a bottle for such news! But how did you come here?"

"I've been sent back to the regiment all on account of that devil, Mack. An Austrian general complained of me. I congratulated him on Mack's arrival... What's the matter, Rostóv? You look as if you'd just come out of a hot bath."

"Oh, my dear fellow, we're in such a stew here these last two days."

The regimental adjutant came in and confirmed the news brought by Zherkóv. They were under orders to advance next day.

"We're going into action, gentlemen!"

"Well, thank God! We've been sitting here too long!"

CHAPTER VI

Kutúzov fell back toward Vienna, destroying behind him the bridges over the rivers Inn (at Braunau) and Traun (near Linz). On October 23 the Russian troops were crossing the river Enns. At midday the Russian baggage train, the artillery, and columns of troops were defiling through the town of Enns on both sides of the bridge.

It was a warm, rainy, autumnal day. The wide expanse that opened out before the heights on which the Russian batteries stood guarding the bridge was at times veiled by a diaphanous curtain of slanting rain, and then, suddenly spread out in the sunlight, far-distant objects could be clearly seen glittering as though freshly varnished. Down below, the little town could be seen with its white, red-roofed houses, its cathedral, and its bridge, on both sides of which streamed jostling masses of Russian troops. At the bend of the Danube, vessels, an island, and a castle with a park surrounded by the waters of the confluence of the Enns and the Danube became visible, and the rocky left bank of the Danube covered with pine forests, with a mystic background of green treetops and bluish gorges. The turrets of a convent stood out beyond a wild virgin pine forest, and far away on the other side of the Enns the enemy's horse patrols could be discerned.

Among the field guns on the brow of the hill the general in command of the rearguard stood with a staff officer, scanning the country through his fieldglass. A little behind them Nesvítski, who had been sent to the rearguard by the commander in chief, was sitting on the trail of a gun carriage. A Cossack who accompanied him had handed him a knapsack and a flask, and Nesvítski was treating some officers to pies and real *doppelkümmel*. The officers gladly gathered round him, some on their knees, some squatting Turkish fashion on the wet grass.

"Yes, the Austrian prince who built that castle was no fool. It's a fine place! Why are you not eating anything, gentlemen?" Nesvítski was saying.

"Thank you very much, Prince," answered one of the officers, pleased to be talking to a staff officer of such importance. "It's a lovely place! We passed close to the park and saw two deer... and what a splendid house!"

"Look, Prince," said another, who would have dearly liked to take another pie but felt shy, and therefore pretended to be examining the countryside—"See, our infantrymen have already got there. Look there in the meadow behind the village, three of them are dragging something. They'll ransack that castle," he remarked with evident approval.

"So they will," said Nesvítski. "No, but what I should like," added he, munching a pie in his moist-lipped handsome mouth, "would be to slip in over there."

He pointed with a smile to a turreted nunnery, and his eyes narrowed and gleamed.

"That would be fine, gentlemen!"

The officers laughed.

"Just to flutter the nuns a bit. They say there are Italian girls among them. On my word I'd give five years of my life for it!"

"They must be feeling dull, too," said one of the bolder officers, laughing.

Meanwhile the staff officer standing in front pointed out something to the general, who looked through his field glass.

"Yes, so it is, so it is," said the general angrily, lowering the field glass and shrugging his shoulders, "so it is! They'll be fired on at the crossing. And why are they dawdling there?"

On the opposite side the enemy could be seen by the naked eye, and from their battery a milk-white cloud arose. Then came the distant report of a shot, and our troops could be seen hurrying to the crossing.

Nesvítski rose, puffing, and went up to the general, smiling.

"Would not your excellency like a little refreshment?" he said.

"It's a bad business," said the general without answering him, "our men have been wasting time."

"Hadn't I better ride over, your excellency?" asked Nesvítski.

"Yes, please do," answered the general, and he repeated the order that had already once been given in detail: "and tell the hussars that they are to cross last and to fire the bridge as I ordered; and the inflammable material on the bridge must be reinspected."

"Very good," answered Nesvítski.

He called the Cossack with his horse, told him to put away the knapsack and flask, and swung his heavy person easily into the saddle.

"I'll really call in on the nuns," he said to the officers who watched him smilingly, and he rode off by the winding path down the hill.

"Now then, let's see how far it will carry, Captain. Just try!" said the general, turning to an artillery officer. "Have a little fun to pass the time."

"Crew, to your guns!" commanded the officer.

In a moment the men came running gaily from their campfires and began loading.

"One!" came the command.

Number one jumped briskly aside. The gun rang out with a deafening metallic roar, and a whistling grenade flew above the heads of our troops below the hill and fell far short of the enemy, a little smoke showing the spot where it burst.

The faces of officers and men brightened up at the sound. Everyone got up and began watching the movements of our troops below, as plainly visible as if but a stone's throw away, and the movements of the approaching enemy farther off. At the same instant the sun came fully out from behind the clouds, and the clear sound of the solitary shot and the brilliance of the bright sunshine merged in a single joyous and spirited impression.

CHAPTER VII

Two of the enemy's shots had already flown across the bridge, where there was a crush. Halfway across stood Prince Nesvítski, who had alighted from his horse and whose big body was jammed against the railings. He looked back laughing to the Cossack who stood a few steps behind him holding two horses by their bridles. Each time Prince Nesvítski tried to move on, soldiers and carts pushed him back again and pressed him against the railings, and all he could do was to smile.

"What a fine fellow you are, friend!" said the Cossack to a convoy soldier with a wagon, who was pressing onto the infantrymen who were crowded together close to his wheels and his horses. "What a fellow! You can't wait a moment! Don't you see the general wants to pass?"

But the convoyman took no notice of the word "general" and shouted at the soldiers who were blocking his way. "Hi there, boys! Keep to the left! Wait a bit." But the soldiers, crowded together shoulder to shoulder, their bayonets interlocking, moved over the bridge in a dense mass. Looking down over the rails Prince Nesvítski saw the rapid, noisy little waves of the Enns, which rippling and eddying round the piles of the bridge chased each other along. Looking on the bridge he saw equally uniform living waves of soldiers, shoulder straps, covered shakos, knapsacks, bayonets, long muskets, and, under the shakos, faces with broad cheekbones, sunken cheeks, and listless tired expressions, and feet that moved through the sticky mud that covered the planks of the bridge. Sometimes through the monotonous waves of men, like a fleck of white foam on the waves of the Enns, an officer, in a cloak and with a type of face different from that of the men, squeezed his way along; sometimes like a chip of wood whirling in the river, an hussar on foot, an orderly, or a townsman was carried through the waves of infantry; and sometimes like a log floating down the river, an officers' or company's baggage wagon, piled high, leather covered, and hemmed in on all sides, moved across the bridge.

"It's as if a dam had burst," said the Cossack hopelessly. "Are there many more of you to come?"

"A million all but one!" replied a waggish soldier in a torn coat, with a wink, and passed on followed by another, an old man.

"If *he*" (*he* meant the enemy) "begins popping at the bridge now," said the old soldier dismally to a comrade, "you'll forget to scratch yourself."

That soldier passed on, and after him came another sitting on a cart.

"Where the devil have the leg bands been shoved to?" said an orderly, running behind the cart and fumbling in the back of it.

And he also passed on with the wagon. Then came some merry soldiers who had evidently been drinking.

"And then, old fellow, he gives him one in the teeth with the butt end of his gun..." a soldier whose greatcoat was well tucked up said gaily, with a wide swing of his arm.

"Yes, the ham was just delicious..." answered another with a loud laugh. And they, too, passed on, so that Nesvítski did not learn who had been struck on the teeth, or what the ham had to do with it.

"Bah! How they scurry. He just sends a ball and they think they'll all be killed," a sergeant was saying angrily and reproachfully.

"As it flies past me, Daddy, the ball I mean," said a young soldier with an enormous mouth, hardly refraining from laughing, "I felt like dying of fright. I did, 'pon my word, I got that frightened!" said he, as if bragging of having been frightened.

That one also passed. Then followed a cart unlike any that had gone before. It was a German cart with a pair of horses led by a German, and seemed loaded with a whole houseful of effects. A fine brindled cow with a large udder was attached to the cart behind. A woman with an unweaned baby, an old woman, and a healthy German girl with bright red cheeks were sitting on some feather beds. Evidently these fugitives were allowed to pass by special permission. The eyes of all the soldiers turned toward the women, and while the vehicle was passing at foot pace all the soldiers' remarks related to the two young ones. Every face bore almost the same smile, expressing unseemly thoughts about the women.

"Just see, the German sausage is making tracks, too!"

"Sell me the missis," said another soldier, addressing the German, who, angry and frightened, strode energetically along with downcast eyes.

"See how smart she's made herself! Oh, the devils!"

"There, Fedótov, you should be quartered on them!"

"I have seen as much before now, mate!"

"Where are you going?" asked an infantry officer who was eating an apple, also half smiling as he looked at the handsome girl.

The German closed his eyes, signifying that he did not understand.

"Take it if you like," said the officer, giving the girl an apple.

The girl smiled and took it. Nesvítski like the rest of the men on the bridge did not take his eyes off the women till they had passed. When they had gone by, the same stream of soldiers followed, with the same kind of talk, and at last all stopped. As often happens, the horses of a convoy wagon became restive at the end of the bridge, and the whole crowd had to wait.

"And why are they stopping? There's no proper order!" said the soldiers. "Where are you shoving to? Devil take you! Can't you wait? It'll be worse if he fires the bridge. See, here's an officer jammed in too"—different voices were saying in the crowd, as the men looked at one another, and all pressed toward the exit from the bridge.

Looking down at the waters of the Enns under the bridge, Nesvítski suddenly heard a sound new to him, of something swiftly approaching... something big, that splashed into the water.

"Just see where it carries to!" a soldier near by said sternly, looking round at the sound.

"Encouraging us to get along quicker," said another uneasily.

The crowd moved on again. Nesvítski realized that it was a cannon ball.

"Hey, Cossack, my horse!" he said. "Now, then, you there! get out of the way! Make way!"

With great difficulty he managed to get to his horse, and shouting continually he moved on. The soldiers squeezed themselves to make way for him, but again pressed on him so that they jammed his leg, and those nearest him were not to blame for they were themselves pressed still harder from behind.

"Nesvítski, Nesvítski! you numskull!" came a hoarse voice from behind him.

Nesvítski looked round and saw, some fifteen paces away but separated by the living mass of moving infantry, VáskaDenísov, red and shaggy, with his cap on the back of his black head and a cloak hanging jauntily over his shoulder.

"Tell these devils, these fiends, to let me pass!" shouted Denísov evidently in a fit of rage, his coal-black eyes with their bloodshot whites glittering and rolling as he waved his sheathed saber in a small bare hand as red as his face.

"Ah, Váska!" joyfully replied Nesvítski. "What's up with you?"

"The squadwon can't pass," shouted VáskaDenísov, showing his white teeth fiercely and spurring his black thoroughbred Arab, which twitched its ears as the bayonets touched it, and snorted, spurting white foam from his bit, tramping the planks of the bridge with his hoofs, and apparently ready to jump over the railings had his rider let him. "What is this? They're like sheep! Just like sheep! Out of the way!... Let us pass!... Stop there, you devil with the cart! I'll hack you with my saber!" he shouted, actually drawing his saber from its scabbard and flourishing it.

The soldiers crowded against one another with terrified faces, and Denísov joined Nesvítski.

"How's it you're not drunk today?" said Nesvítski when the other had ridden up to him.

"They don't even give one time to dwink!" answered VáskaDenísov. "They keep dwagging the wegiment to and fwo all day. If they mean to fight, let's fight. But the devil knows what this is."

"What a dandy you are today!" said Nesvítski, looking at Denísov's new cloak and saddlecloth.

Denísov smiled, took out of his sabretache a handkerchief that diffused a smell of perfume, and put it to Nesvítski's nose.

"Of course. I'm going into action! I've shaved, bwushed my teeth, and scented myself."

The imposing figure of Nesvítski followed by his Cossack, and the determination of Denísov who flourished his sword and shouted frantically, had such an effect that they managed to squeeze through to the farther side of the bridge and stopped the infantry. Beside the bridge Nesvítski found the colonel to whom he had to deliver the order, and having done this he rode back.

Having cleared the way Denísov stopped at the end of the bridge. Carelessly holding in his stallion that was neighing and pawing the ground, eager to rejoin its fellows, he watched his squadron draw nearer. Then the clang of hoofs, as of several horses galloping, resounded on the planks of the bridge, and the squadron, officers in front and men four abreast, spread across the bridge and began to emerge on his side of it.

The infantry who had been stopped crowded near the bridge in the trampled mud and gazed with that particular feeling of ill-will, estrangement, and ridicule with which troops of different arms usually encounter one another at the clean, smart hussars who moved past them in regular order.

"Smart lads! Only fit for a fair!" said one.

"What good are they? They're led about just for show!" remarked another.

"Don't kick up the dust, you infantry!" jested an hussar whose prancing horse had splashed mud over some foot soldiers.

"I'd like to put you on a two days' march with a knapsack! Your fine cords would soon get a bit rubbed," said an infantryman, wiping the mud off his face with his sleeve. "Perched up there, you're more like a bird than a man."

"There now, Zíkin, they ought to put you on a horse. You'd look fine," said a corporal, chaffing a thin little soldier who bent under the weight of his knapsack.

"Take a stick between your legs, that'll suit you for a horse!" the hussar shouted back.

CHAPTER VIII

The last of the infantry hurriedly crossed the bridge, squeezing together as they approached it as if passing through a funnel. At last the baggage wagons had all crossed, the crush was less, and the last battalion came onto the bridge. Only Denísov's squadron of hussars remained on the farther side of the bridge facing the enemy, who could be seen from the hill on the opposite bank but was not yet visible from the bridge, for the horizon as seen from the valley through which the river flowed was formed by the rising ground only half a mile away. At the foot of the hill lay wasteland over which a few groups of our Cossack scouts were moving. Suddenly on the road at the top of the high ground, artillery and troops in blue uniform were seen. These were the French. A group of Cossack scouts retired down the hill at a trot. All the officers and men of Denísov's squadron, though they tried to talk of other things and to look in other directions, thought only of what was there on the hilltop, and kept constantly looking at the patches appearing on the skyline, which they knew to be the enemy's troops. The weather had cleared again since noon and the sun was descending brightly upon the Danube and the dark hills around it. It was calm, and at intervals the bugle calls and the shouts of the enemy could be heard from the hill. There was no one now between the squadron and the enemy except a few scattered skirmishers. An empty space of some seven hundred yards was all that separated them. The enemy ceased firing, and that stern, threatening, inaccessible, and intangible line which separates two hostile armies was all the more clearly felt.

"One step beyond that boundary line which resembles the line dividing the living from the dead lies uncertainty, suffering, and death.

And what is there? Who is there?—there beyond that field, that tree, that roof lit up by the sun? No one knows, but one wants to know. You fear and yet long to cross that line, and know that sooner or later it must be crossed and you will have to find out what is there, just as you will inevitably have to learn what lies the other side of death. But you are strong, healthy, cheerful, and excited, and are surrounded by other such excitedly animated and healthy men." So thinks, or at any rate feels, anyone who comes in sight of the enemy, and that feeling gives a particular glamour and glad keenness of impression to everything that takes place at such moments.

On the high ground where the enemy was, the smoke of a cannon rose, and a ball flew whistling over the heads of the hussar squadron. The officers who had been standing together rode off to their places. The hussars began carefully aligning their horses. Silence fell on the whole squadron. All were looking at the enemy in front and at the squadron commander, awaiting the word of command. A second and a third cannon ball flew past. Evidently they were firing at the hussars, but the balls with rapid rhythmic whistle flew over the heads of the horsemen and fell somewhere beyond them. The hussars did not look round, but at the sound of each shot, as at the word of command, the whole squadron with its rows of faces so alike yet so different, holding its breath while the ball flew past, rose in the stirrups and sank back again. The soldiers without turning their heads glanced at one another, curious to see their comrades' impression. Every face, from Denísov's to that of the bugler, showed one common expression of conflict, irritation, and excitement, around chin and mouth. The quartermaster frowned, looking at the soldiers as if threatening to punish them. Cadet Mirónov ducked every time a ball flew past. Rostóv on the left flank, mounted on his Rook—a handsome horse despite its game leg—had the happy air of a schoolboy called up before a large audience for an examination in which he feels sure he will distinguish himself. He was glancing at everyone with a clear, bright expression, as if asking them to notice how calmly he sat under fire. But despite himself, on his face too that same indication of something new and stern showed round the mouth.

"Who's that curtseying there? Cadet Miwónov! That's not wight! Look at me," cried Denísov who, unable to keep still on one spot, kept turning his horse in front of the squadron.

The black, hairy, snub-nosed face of VáskaDenísov, and his whole short sturdy figure with the sinewy hairy hand and stumpy fingers in which he held the hilt of his naked saber, looked just as it usually did, especially toward evening when he had emptied his second bottle; he was only redder than usual. With his shaggy head thrown back like birds when they drink, pressing his spurs mercilessly into the sides of his good horse, Bedouin, and sitting as though falling backwards in the saddle, he galloped to the other flank of the squadron and shouted in a hoarse voice to the men to look to their pistols. He rode up to Kírsten. The staff captain on his broad-backed, steady mare came at a walk to meet him. His face with its long mustache was serious as always, only his eyes were brighter than usual.

"Well, what about it?" said he to Denísov. "It won't come to a fight. You'll see—we shall retire."

"The devil only knows what they're about!" muttered Denísov. "Ah, Wostóv," he cried noticing the cadet's bright face, "you've got it at last."

And he smiled approvingly, evidently pleased with the cadet. Rostóv felt perfectly happy. Just then the commander appeared on the bridge. Denísov galloped up to him.

"Your excellency! Let us attack them! I'll dwive them off."

"Attack indeed!" said the colonel in a bored voice, puckering up his face as if driving off a troublesome fly. "And why are you stopping here? Don't you see the skirmishers are retreating? Lead the squadron back."

The squadron crossed the bridge and drew out of range of fire without having lost a single man. The second squadron that had been in the front line followed them across and the last Cossacks quitted the farther side of the river.

The two Pávlograd squadrons, having crossed the bridge, retired up the hill one after the other. Their colonel, Karl Bogdánich Schubert, came up to Denísov's squadron and rode at a footpace not far from Rostóv, without taking any notice of him although they were now meeting for the first time since their encounter concerning Telyánin. Rostóv, feeling that he was at the front and in the power of a man toward whom he now admitted that he had been to blame, did not lift his eyes from the colonel's athletic back, his nape covered with light hair, and his red neck. It seemed to Rostóv that Bogdánich was only pretending not to notice him, and that his whole aim now was to test the cadet's courage, so he drew himself up and looked around him merrily; then it seemed to him that Bogdánich rode so near in order to show him his courage. Next he thought that his enemy would send the squadron on a desperate attack just to punish him—Rostóv. Then he imagined how, after the attack, Bogdánich would come up to him as he lay wounded and would magnanimously extend the hand of reconciliation.

The high-shouldered figure of Zherkóv, familiar to the Pávlograds as he had but recently left their regiment, rode up to the colonel. After his dismissal from headquarters Zherkóv had not remained in the regiment, saying he was not such a fool as to slave at the front when he could get more rewards by doing nothing on the staff, and had succeeded in attaching himself as an orderly officer to Prince Bagratión. He now came to his former chief with an order from the commander of the rear guard.

"Colonel," he said, addressing Rostóv's enemy with an air of gloomy gravity and glancing round at his comrades, "there is an order to stop and fire the bridge."

"An order to who?" asked the colonel morosely.

"I don't myself know 'to who,'" replied the cornet in a serious tone, "but the prince told me to 'go and tell the colonel that the hussars must return quickly and fire the bridge.'"

Zherkóv was followed by an officer of the suite who rode up to the colonel of hussars with the same order. After him the stout Nesvítski came galloping up on a Cossack horse that could scarcely carry his weight.

"How's this, Colonel?" he shouted as he approached. "I told you to fire the bridge, and now someone has gone and blundered; they are all beside themselves over there and one can't make anything out."

The colonel deliberately stopped the regiment and turned to Nesvítski.

"You spoke to me of inflammable material," said he, "but you said nothing about firing it."

"But, my dear sir," said Nesvítski as he drew up, taking off his cap and smoothing his hair wet with perspiration with his plump hand, "wasn't I telling you to fire the bridge, when inflammable material had been put in position?"

"I am not your 'dear sir,' Mr. Staff Officer, and you did not tell me to burn the bridge! I know the service, and it is my habit orders strictly to obey. You said the bridge would be burned, but who would burn it, I could not know by the holy spirit!"

"Ah, that's always the way!" said Nesvítski with a wave of the hand. "How did you get here?" said he, turning to Zherkóv.

"On the same business. But you *are* damp! Let me wring you out!"

"You were saying, Mr. Staff Officer..." continued the colonel in an offended tone.

"Colonel," interrupted the officer of the suite, "You must be quick or the enemy will bring up his guns to use grapeshot."

The colonel looked silently at the officer of the suite, at the stout staff officer, and at Zherkóv, and he frowned.

"I will the bridge fire," he said in a solemn tone as if to announce that in spite of all the unpleasantness he had to endure he would still do the right thing.

Striking his horse with his long muscular legs as if it were to blame for everything, the colonel moved forward and ordered the second squadron, that in which Rostóv was serving under Denísov, to return to the bridge.

"There, it's just as I thought," said Rostóv to himself. "He wishes to test me!" His heart contracted and the blood rushed to his face. "Let him see whether I am a coward!" he thought.

Again on all the bright faces of the squadron the serious expression appeared that they had worn when under fire. Rostóv watched his enemy, the colonel, closely—to find in his face confirmation of his own conjecture, but the colonel did not once glance at Rostóv, and looked as he always did when at the front, solemn and stern. Then came the word of command.

"Look sharp! Look sharp!" several voices repeated around him.

Their sabers catching in the bridles and their spurs jingling, the hussars hastily dismounted, not knowing what they were to do.

The men were crossing themselves. Rostóv no longer looked at the colonel, he had no time. He was afraid of falling behind the hussars, so much afraid that his heart stood still. His hand trembled as he gave his horse into an orderly's charge, and he felt the blood rush to his heart with a thud. Denísov rode past him, leaning back and shouting something. Rostóv saw nothing but the hussars running all around him, their spurs catching and their sabers clattering.

"Stretchers!" shouted someone behind him.

Rostóv did not think what this call for stretchers meant; he ran on, trying only to be ahead of the others; but just at the bridge, not looking at the ground, he came on some sticky, trodden mud, stumbled, and fell on his hands. The others outstripped him.

"At boss zides, Captain," he heard the voice of the colonel, who, having ridden ahead, had pulled up his horse near the bridge, with a triumphant, cheerful face.

Rostóv wiping his muddy hands on his breeches looked at his enemy and was about to run on, thinking that the farther he went to the front the better. But Bogdánich, without looking at or recognizing Rostóv, shouted to him:

"Who's that running on the middle of the bridge? To the right! Come back, Cadet!" he cried angrily; and turning to Denísov, who, showing off his courage, had ridden on to the planks of the bridge:

"Why run risks, Captain? You should dismount," he said.

"Oh, every bullet has its billet," answered VáskaDenísov, turning in his saddle.

Meanwhile Nesvítski, Zherkóv, and the officer of the suite were standing together out of range of the shots, watching, now the small group of men with yellow shakos, dark-green jackets braided with cord, and blue riding breeches, who were swarming near the bridge, and then at what was approaching in the distance from the opposite side—the blue uniforms and groups with horses, easily recognizable as artillery.

"Will they burn the bridge or not? Who'll get there first? Will they get there and fire the bridge or will the French get within grapeshot range and wipe them out?" These were the questions each man of the troops on the high ground above the bridge involuntarily asked himself with a sinking heart—watching the bridge and the hussars in the bright evening light and the blue tunics advancing from the other side with their bayonets and guns.

"Ugh. The hussars will get it hot!" said Nesvítski; "they are within grapeshot range now."

"He shouldn't have taken so many men," said the officer of the suite.

"True enough," answered Nesvítski; "two smart fellows could have done the job just as well."

"Ah, your excellency," put in Zherkóv, his eyes fixed on the hussars, but still with that naïve air that made it impossible to know whether he was speaking in jest or in earnest. "Ah, your excellency! How you look at things! Send two men? And who then would give us the Vladímir medal and ribbon? But now, even if they do get peppered, the squadron may be recommended for honors and he may get a ribbon. Our Bogdánich knows how things are done."

"There now!" said the officer of the suite, "that's grapeshot."

He pointed to the French guns, the limbers of which were being detached and hurriedly removed.

On the French side, amid the groups with cannon, a cloud of smoke appeared, then a second and a third almost simultaneously, and at the moment when the first report was heard a fourth was seen. Then two reports one after another, and a third.

"Oh! Oh!" groaned Nesvítski as if in fierce pain, seizing the officer of the suite by the arm. "Look! A man has fallen! Fallen, fallen!"

"Two, I think."

"If I were Tsar I would never go to war," said Nesvítski, turning away.

The French guns were hastily reloaded. The infantry in their blue uniforms advanced toward the bridge at a run. Smoke appeared again but at irregular intervals, and grapeshot cracked and rattled onto the bridge. But this time Nesvítski could not see what was happening there, as a dense cloud of smoke arose from it. The hussars had succeeded in setting it on fire and the French batteries were now firing at them, no longer to hinder them but because the guns were trained and there was someone to fire at.

The French had time to fire three rounds of grapeshot before the hussars got back to their horses. Two were misdirected and the shot went too high, but the last round fell in the midst of a group of hussars and knocked three of them over.

Rostóv, absorbed by his relations with Bogdánich, had paused on the bridge not knowing what to do. There was no one to hew down (as he had always imagined battles to himself), nor could he help to fire the bridge because he had not brought any burning straw with him like the other soldiers. He stood looking about him, when suddenly he heard a rattle on the bridge as if nuts were being spilt, and the hussar nearest to him fell against the rails with a groan. Rostóv ran up to him with the others. Again someone shouted, "Stretchers!" Four men seized the hussar and began lifting him.

"Oooh! For Christ's sake let me alone!" cried the wounded man, but still he was lifted and laid on the stretcher.

Nicholas Rostóv turned away and, as if searching for something, gazed into the distance, at the waters of the Danube, at the sky, and at the sun. How beautiful the sky looked; how blue, how calm, and how deep! How bright and glorious was the setting sun! With what soft glitter the waters of the distant Danube shone. And fairer still were the faraway blue mountains beyond the river, the nunnery, the mysterious gorges, and the pine forests veiled in the mist of their summits... There was peace and happiness... "I should wish for nothing else, nothing, if only I were there," thought Rostóv. "In myself alone and in that sunshine there is so much happiness; but here... groans, suffering, fear, and this uncertainty and hurry... There—they are shouting again, and again are all running back somewhere, and I shall run with them, and it, death, is here above me and around... Another instant and I shall never again see the sun, this water, that gorge!..."

At that instant the sun began to hide behind the clouds, and other stretchers came into view before Rostóv. And the fear of death and of the stretchers, and love of the sun and of life, all merged into one feeling of sickening agitation.

"O Lord God! Thou who art in that heaven, save, forgive, and protect me!" Rostóv whispered.

The hussars ran back to the men who held their horses; their voices sounded louder and calmer, the stretchers disappeared from sight.

"Well, fwiend? So you've smelt powdah!" shouted VáskaDenísov just above his ear.

"It's all over; but I am a coward—yes, a coward!" thought Rostóv, and sighing deeply he took Rook, his horse, which stood resting one foot, from the orderly and began to mount.

"Was that grapeshot?" he asked Denísov.

"Yes and no mistake!" cried Denísov. "You worked like wegularbwicks and it's nasty work! An attack's pleasant work! Hacking away at the dogs! But this sort of thing is the very devil, with them shooting at you like a target."

And Denísov rode up to a group that had stopped near Rostóv, composed of the colonel, Nesvítski, Zherkóv, and the officer from the suite.

"Well, it seems that no one has noticed," thought Rostóv. And this was true. No one had taken any notice, for everyone knew the sensation which the cadet under fire for the first time had experienced.

"Here's something for you to report," said Zherkóv. "See if I don't get promoted to a sublieutenancy."

"Inform the prince that I the bridge fired!" said the colonel triumphantly and gaily.

"And if he asks about the losses?"

"A trifle," said the colonel in his bass voice: "two hussars wounded, and one knocked out," he added, unable to restrain a happy smile, and pronouncing the phrase "knocked out" with ringing distinctness.

CHAPTER IX

Pursued by the French army of a hundred thousand men under the command of Bonaparte, encountering a population that was unfriendly to it, losing confidence in its allies, suffering from shortness of supplies, and compelled to act under conditions of war unlike anything that had been foreseen, the Russian army of thirty-five thousand men commanded by Kutúzov was hurriedly retreating along the Danube, stopping where overtaken by the enemy and fighting rearguard actions only as far as necessary to enable it to retreat without losing its heavy equipment. There had been actions at Lambach, Amstetten, and Melk; but despite the courage and endurance—acknowledged even by the enemy—with which the Russians fought, the only consequence of these actions was a yet more rapid retreat. Austrian troops that had escaped capture at Ulm and had joined Kutúzov at Braunau now separated from the Russian army, and Kutúzov was left with only his own weak and exhausted forces. The defense of Vienna was no longer to be thought of. Instead of an offensive, the plan of which, carefully prepared in accord with the modern science of strategics, had been handed to Kutúzov when he was in Vienna by the Austrian Hofkriegsrath, the sole and almost unattainable aim remaining for him was to effect a junction with the forces that were advancing from Russia, without losing his army as Mack had done at Ulm.

On the twenty-eighth of October Kutúzov with his army crossed to the left bank of the Danube and took up a position for the first time with the river between himself and the main body of the French. On the thirtieth he attacked Mortier's division, which was on the left bank, and broke it up. In this action for the first time trophies were taken:

banners, cannon, and two enemy generals. For the first time, after a fortnight's retreat, the Russian troops had halted and after a fight had not only held the field but had repulsed the French. Though the troops were ill-clad, exhausted, and had lost a third of their number in killed, wounded, sick, and stragglers; though a number of sick and wounded had been abandoned on the other side of the Danube with a letter in which Kutúzov entrusted them to the humanity of the enemy; and though the big hospitals and the houses in Krems converted into military hospitals could no longer accommodate all the sick and wounded, yet the stand made at Krems and the victory over Mortier raised the spirits of the army considerably. Throughout the whole army and at headquarters most joyful though erroneous rumors were rife of the imaginary approach of columns from Russia, of some victory gained by the Austrians, and of the retreat of the frightened Bonaparte.

Prince Andrew during the battle had been in attendance on the Austrian General Schmidt, who was killed in the action. His horse had been wounded under him and his own arm slightly grazed by a bullet. As a mark of the commander in chief's special favor he was sent with the news of this victory to the Austrian court, now no longer at Vienna (which was threatened by the French) but at Brünn. Despite his apparently delicate build Prince Andrew could endure physical fatigue far better than many very muscular men, and on the night of the battle, having arrived at Krems excited but not weary, with dispatches from Dokhtúrov to Kutúzov, he was sent immediately with a special dispatch to Brünn. To be so sent meant not only a reward but an important step toward promotion.

The night was dark but starry, the road showed black in the snow that had fallen the previous day—the day of the battle. Reviewing his impressions of the recent battle, picturing pleasantly to himself the impression his news of a victory would create, or recalling the send-off given him by the commander in chief and his fellow officers, Prince Andrew was galloping along in a post chaise enjoying the feelings of a man who has at length begun to attain a long-desired happiness. As soon as he closed his eyes his ears seemed filled with the rattle of the wheels and the sensation of victory. Then he began to imagine that the Russians were running away and that he himself was killed, but he quickly roused himself with a feeling of joy, as if learning afresh that this was not so but that on the contrary the French had run away. He again recalled all the details of the victory and his own calm courage during the battle, and feeling reassured he dozed off.... The dark starry night was followed by a bright cheerful morning. The snow was thawing in the sunshine, the horses galloped quickly, and on both sides of the road were forests of different kinds, fields, and villages.

At one of the post stations he overtook a convoy of Russian wounded. The Russian officer in charge of the transport lolled back in the front cart, shouting and scolding a soldier with coarse abuse. In each of the long German carts six or more pale, dirty, bandaged men were being jolted over the stony road. Some of them were talking (he heard Russian words), others were eating bread; the more severely wounded looked silently, with the languid interest of sick children, at the envoy hurrying past them.

Prince Andrew told his driver to stop, and asked a soldier in what action they had been wounded. "Day before yesterday, on the Danube," answered the soldier. Prince Andrew took out his purse and gave the soldier three gold pieces.

"That's for them all," he said to the officer who came up.

"Get well soon, lads!" he continued, turning to the soldiers. "There's plenty to do still."

"What news, sir?" asked the officer, evidently anxious to start a conversation.

"Good news!... Go on!" he shouted to the driver, and they galloped on.

It was already quite dark when Prince Andrew rattled over the paved streets of Brünn and found himself surrounded by high buildings, the lights of shops, houses, and street lamps, fine carriages, and all that atmosphere of a large and active town which is always so attractive to a soldier after camp life. Despite his rapid journey and sleepless night, Prince Andrew when he drove up to the palace felt even more vigorous and alert than he had done the day before. Only his eyes gleamed feverishly and his thoughts followed one another with extraordinary clearness and rapidity. He again vividly recalled the details of the battle, no longer dim, but definite and in the concise form in which he imagined himself stating them to the Emperor Francis. He vividly imagined the casual questions that might be put to him and the answers he would give. He expected to be at once presented to the Emperor. At the chief entrance to the palace, however, an official came running out to meet him, and learning that he was a special messenger led him to another entrance.

"To the right from the corridor, *EuerHochgeboren!* There you will find the adjutant on duty," said the official. "He will conduct you to the Minister of War."

The adjutant on duty, meeting Prince Andrew, asked him to wait, and went in to the Minister of War. Five minutes later he returned and bowing with particular courtesy ushered Prince Andrew before him along a corridor to the cabinet where the Minister of War was at work. The adjutant by his elaborate courtesy appeared to wish to ward off any attempt at familiarity on the part of the Russian messenger.

Prince Andrew's joyous feeling was considerably weakened as he approached the door of the minister's room. He felt offended, and without his noticing it the feeling of offense immediately turned into one of disdain which was quite uncalled for. His fertile mind instantly suggested to him a point of view which gave him a right to despise the adjutant and the minister. "Away from the smell of powder, they probably think it easy to gain victories!" he thought. His eyes narrowed disdainfully, he entered the room of the Minister of War with peculiarly deliberate steps. This feeling of disdain was heightened when he saw the minister seated at a large table reading some papers and making pencil notes on them, and for the first two or three minutes taking no notice of his arrival. A wax candle stood at each side of the minister's bent bald head with its gray temples. He went on reading to the end, without raising his eyes at the opening of the door and the sound of footsteps.

"Take this and deliver it," said he to his adjutant, handing him the papers and still taking no notice of the special messenger.

Prince Andrew felt that either the actions of Kutúzov's army interested the Minister of War less than any of the other matters he was concerned with, or he wanted to give the Russian special messenger that impression. "But that is a matter of perfect indifference to me," he thought. The minister drew the remaining papers together, arranged them evenly, and then raised his head. He had an intellectual and distinctive head, but the instant he turned to Prince Andrew the firm, intelligent expression on his face changed in a way evidently deliberate and habitual to him. His face took on the stupid artificial smile (which does not even attempt to hide its artificiality) of a man who is continually receiving many petitioners one after another.

"From General Field Marshal Kutúzov?" he asked. "I hope it is good news? There has been an encounter with Mortier? A victory? It was high time!"

He took the dispatch which was addressed to him and began to read it with a mournful expression.

"Oh, my God! My God! Schmidt!" he exclaimed in German. "What a calamity! What a calamity!"

Having glanced through the dispatch he laid it on the table and looked at Prince Andrew, evidently considering something.

"Ah what a calamity! You say the affair was decisive? But Mortier is not captured." Again he pondered. "I am very glad you have brought good news, though Schmidt's death is a heavy price to pay for the victory. His Majesty will no doubt wish to see you, but not today. I thank you! You must have a rest. Be at the levee tomorrow after the parade. However, I will let you know."

The stupid smile, which had left his face while he was speaking, reappeared.

"*Au revoir!* Thank you very much. His Majesty will probably desire to see you," he added, bowing his head.

When Prince Andrew left the palace he felt that all the interest and happiness the victory had afforded him had been now left in the indifferent hands of the Minister of War and the polite adjutant. The whole tenor of his thoughts instantaneously changed; the battle seemed the memory of a remote event long past.

CHAPTER X

Prince Andrew stayed at Brünn with Bilíbin, a Russian acquaintance of his in the diplomatic service.

"Ah, my dear prince! I could not have a more welcome visitor," said Bilíbin as he came out to meet Prince Andrew. "Franz, put the prince's things in my bedroom," said he to the servant who was ushering Bolkónski in. "So you're a messenger of victory, eh? Splendid! And I am sitting here ill, as you see."

After washing and dressing, Prince Andrew came into the diplomat's luxurious study and sat down to the dinner prepared for him. Bilíbin settled down comfortably beside the fire.

After his journey and the campaign during which he had been deprived of all the comforts of cleanliness and all the refinements of life, Prince Andrew felt a pleasant sense of repose among luxurious surroundings such as he had been accustomed to from childhood. Besides it was pleasant, after his reception by the Austrians, to speak if not in Russian (for they were speaking French) at least with a Russian who would, he supposed, share the general Russian antipathy to the Austrians which was then particularly strong.

Bilíbin was a man of thirty-five, a bachelor, and of the same circle as Prince Andrew. They had known each other previously in Petersburg, but had become more intimate when Prince Andrew was in Vienna with Kutúzov. Just as Prince Andrew was a young man who gave promise of rising high in the military profession, so to an even greater extent Bilíbin gave promise of rising in his diplomatic career. He was still a young man but no longer a young diplomat, as he had entered the service at the age of sixteen, had been in Paris and Copenhagen, and now held a rather important post in Vienna. Both the foreign minister and our ambassador in Vienna knew him and valued him. He was not one of those many diplomats who are esteemed because they have certain negative qualities, avoid doing certain things, and speak French. He was one of those, who, liking work, knew how to do it, and despite his indolence would sometimes spend a whole night at his writing table. He worked well whatever the import of his work. It was not the question "What for?" but the question "How?" that interested him. What the diplomatic matter might be he did not care, but it gave him great pleasure to prepare a circular, memorandum, or report, skillfully, pointedly, and elegantly. Bilíbin's services were valued not only for what he wrote, but also for his skill in dealing and conversing with those in the highest spheres.

Bilíbin liked conversation as he liked work, only when it could be made elegantly witty. In society he always awaited an opportunity to say something striking and took part in a conversation only when that was possible. His conversation was always sprinkled with wittily original, finished phrases of general interest. These sayings were prepared in the inner laboratory of his mind in a portable form as if intentionally, so that insignificant society people might carry them from drawing room to drawing room. And, in fact, Bilíbin's witticisms were hawked about in the Viennese drawing rooms and often had an influence on matters considered important.

His thin, worn, sallow face was covered with deep wrinkles, which always looked as clean and well washed as the tips of one's fingers after a Russian bath. The movement of these wrinkles formed the principal play of expression on his face. Now his forehead would pucker into deep folds and his eyebrows were lifted, then his eyebrows would descend and deep wrinkles would crease his cheeks. His small, deep-set eyes always twinkled and looked out straight.

"Well, now tell me about your exploits," said he.

Bolkónski, very modestly without once mentioning himself, described the engagement and his reception by the Minister of War.

"They received me and my news as one receives a dog in a game of skittles," said he in conclusion.

Bilíbin smiled and the wrinkles on his face disappeared.

"Cependant, moncher," he remarked, examining his nails from a distance and puckering the skin above his left eye, *"malgré la haute*

estime que jeprofesse pour the Orthodox Russian army, *j'avoue que votrevictoiren'est pas des plus victorieuses."* *

* "But my dear fellow, with all my respect for the Orthodox Russian army, I must say that your victory was not particularly victorious."

He went on talking in this way in French, uttering only those words in Russian on which he wished to put a contemptuous emphasis.

"Come now! You with all your forces fall on the unfortunate Mortier and his one division, and even then Mortier slips through your fingers! Where's the victory?"

"But seriously," said Prince Andrew, "we can at any rate say without boasting that it was a little better than at Ulm..."

"Why didn't you capture one, just one, marshal for us?"

"Because not everything happens as one expects or with the smoothness of a parade. We had expected, as I told you, to get at their rear by seven in the morning but had not reached it by five in the afternoon."

"And why didn't you do it at seven in the morning? You ought to have been there at seven in the morning," returned Bilíbin with a smile. "You ought to have been there at seven in the morning."

"Why did you not succeed in impressing on Bonaparte by diplomatic methods that he had better leave Genoa alone?" retorted Prince Andrew in the same tone.

"I know," interrupted Bilíbin, "you're thinking it's very easy to take marshals, sitting on a sofa by the fire! That is true, but still why didn't you capture him? So don't be surprised if not only the Minister of War but also his Most August Majesty the Emperor and King Francis is not much delighted by your victory. Even I, a poor secretary of the Russian Embassy, do not feel any need in token of my joy to give my Franz a thaler, or let him go with his *Liebchen* to the Prater... True, we have no Prater here..."

He looked straight at Prince Andrew and suddenly unwrinkled his forehead.

"It is now my turn to ask you 'why?' *moncher*," said Bolkónski. "I confess I do not understand: perhaps there are diplomatic subtleties here beyond my feeble intelligence, but I can't make it out. Mack loses a whole army, the Archduke Ferdinand and the Archduke Karl give no signs of life and make blunder after blunder. Kutúzov alone at last gains a real victory, destroying the spell of the invincibility of the French, and the Minister of War does not even care to hear the details."

"That's just it, my dear fellow. You see it's *hurrah* for the Tsar, for Russia, for the Orthodox Greek faith! All that is beautiful, but what do we, I mean the Austrian court, care for your victories? Bring us nice news of a victory by the Archduke Karl or Ferdinand (one archduke's as good as another, as you know) and even if it is only over a fire brigade of Bonaparte's, that will be another story and we'll fire off some cannon! But this sort of thing seems done on purpose to vex us. The Archduke Karl does nothing, the Archduke Ferdinand disgraces himself. You abandon Vienna, give up its defense—as much as to say: 'Heaven is with us, but heaven help you and your capital!' The one general whom we all loved, Schmidt, you expose to a bullet, and then you congratulate us on the victory! Admit that more irritating news than yours could not have been conceived. It's as if it had been done on purpose, on purpose. Besides, suppose you did gain a brilliant victory, if even the Archduke Karl gained a victory, what effect would that have on the general course of events? It's too late now when Vienna is occupied by the French army!"

"What? Occupied? Vienna occupied?"

"Not only occupied, but Bonaparte is at Schönbrunn, and the count, our dear Count Vrbna, goes to him for orders."

After the fatigues and impressions of the journey, his reception, and especially after having dined, Bolkónski felt that he could not take in the full significance of the words he heard.

"Count Lichtenfels was here this morning," Bilíbin continued, "and showed me a letter in which the parade of the French in Vienna was fully described: Prince Murat *et tout le tremblement*... You see that your victory is not a matter for great rejoicing and that you can't be received as a savior."

"Really I don't care about that, I don't care at all," said Prince Andrew, beginning to understand that his news of the battle before Krems was really of small importance in view of such events as the fall of Austria's capital. "How is it Vienna was taken? What of the bridge and its celebrated bridgehead and Prince Auersperg? We heard reports that Prince Auersperg was defending Vienna?" he said.

"Prince Auersperg is on this, on our side of the river, and is defending us—doing it very badly, I think, but still he is defending us. But Vienna is on the other side. No, the bridge has not yet been taken and I hope it will not be, for it is mined and orders have been given to blow it up. Otherwise we should long ago have been in the mountains of Bohemia, and you and your army would have spent a bad quarter of an hour between two fires."

"But still this does not mean that the campaign is over," said Prince Andrew.

"Well, I think it is. The bigwigs here think so too, but they daren't say so. It will be as I said at the beginning of the campaign, it won't be your skirmishing at Dürrenstein, or gunpowder at all, that will decide the matter, but those who devised it," said Bilíbin quoting one of his own mots, releasing the wrinkles on his forehead, and pausing. "The only question is what will come of the meeting between the Emperor Alexander and the King of Prussia in Berlin? If Prussia joins the Allies, Austria's hand will be forced and there will be war. If not it is merely a question of settling where the preliminaries of the new Campo Formio are to be drawn up."

"What an extraordinary genius!" Prince Andrew suddenly exclaimed, clenching his small hand and striking the table with it, "and what luck the man has!"

"Buonaparte?" said Bilíbin inquiringly, puckering up his forehead to indicate that he was about to say something witty. "Buonaparte?" he repeated, accentuating the *u*: "I think, however, now that he lays down laws for Austria at Schönbrunn, *il faut lui faire grâce de l'u!* * I shall certainly adopt an innovation and call him simply Bonaparte!"

* "We must let him off the u!"

"But joking apart," said Prince Andrew, "do you really think the campaign is over?"

"This is what I think. Austria has been made a fool of, and she is not used to it. She will retaliate. And she has been fooled in the first place because her provinces have been pillaged—they say the Holy Russian army loots terribly—her army is destroyed, her capital taken, and all this for the *beaux yeux* * of His Sardinian Majesty. And therefore—this is between ourselves—I instinctively feel that we are being deceived, my instinct tells me of negotiations with France and projects for peace, a secret peace concluded separately."

* Fine eyes.

"Impossible!" cried Prince Andrew. "That would be too base."

"If we live we shall see," replied Bilíbin, his face again becoming smooth as a sign that the conversation was at an end.

When Prince Andrew reached the room prepared for him and lay down in a clean shirt on the feather bed with its warmed and fragrant pillows, he felt that the battle of which he had brought tidings was far, far away from him. The alliance with Prussia, Austria's treachery, Bonaparte's new triumph, tomorrow's levee and parade, and the audience with the Emperor Francis occupied his thoughts.

He closed his eyes, and immediately a sound of cannonading, of musketry and the rattling of carriage wheels seemed to fill his ears, and now again drawn out in a thin line the musketeers were descending the hill, the French were firing, and he felt his heart palpitating as he rode forward beside Schmidt with the bullets merrily whistling all around, and he experienced tenfold the joy of living, as he had not done since childhood.

He woke up...

"Yes, that all happened!" he said, and, smiling happily to himself like a child, he fell into a deep, youthful slumber.

CHAPTER XI

Next day he woke late. Recalling his recent impressions, the first thought that came into his mind was that today he had to be presented to the Emperor Francis; he remembered the Minister of War, the polite Austrian adjutant, Bilíbin, and last night's conversation. Having dressed for his attendance at court in full parade uniform, which he had not worn for a long time, he went into Bilíbin's study fresh, animated, and handsome, with his hand bandaged. In the study were four gentlemen of the diplomatic corps. With Prince Hippolyte Kurágin, who was a secretary to the embassy, Bolkónski was already acquainted. Bilíbin introduced him to the others.

The gentlemen assembled at Bilíbin's were young, wealthy, gay society men, who here, as in Vienna, formed a special set which Bilíbin, their leader, called *les nôtres*. * This set, consisting almost exclusively of diplomats, evidently had its own interests which had nothing to do with war or politics but related to high society, to certain women, and to the official side of the service. These gentlemen received Prince Andrew as one of themselves, an honor they did not extend to many. From politeness and to start conversation, they asked him a few questions about the army and the battle, and then the talk went off into merry jests and gossip.

* Ours.

"But the best of it was," said one, telling of the misfortune of a fellow diplomat, "that the Chancellor told him flatly that his appointment to London was a promotion and that he was so to regard it. Can you fancy the figure he cut?..."

"But the worst of it, gentlemen—I am giving Kuráginaway to you—is that that man suffers, and this Don Juan, wicked fellow, is taking advantage of it!"

Prince Hippolyte was lolling in a lounge chair with his legs over its arm. He began to laugh.

"Tell me about that!" he said.

"Oh, you Don Juan! You serpent!" cried several voices.

"You, Bolkónski, don't know," said Bilíbin turning to Prince Andrew, "that all the atrocities of the French army (I nearly said of the Russian army) are nothing compared to what this man has been doing among the women!"

"La femme est la compagne de l'homme," * announced Prince Hippolyte, and began looking through a lorgnette at his elevated legs.

* "Woman is man's companion."

Bilíbin and the rest of "ours" burst out laughing in Hippolyte's face, and Prince Andrew saw that Hippolyte, of whom—he had to admit—he had almost been jealous on his wife's account, was the butt of this set.

"Oh, I must give you a treat," Bilíbin whispered to Bolkónski. "Kurágin is exquisite when he discusses politics—you should see his gravity!"

He sat down beside Hippolyte and wrinkling his forehead began talking to him about politics. Prince Andrew and the others gathered round these two.

"The Berlin cabinet cannot express a feeling of alliance," began Hippolyte gazing round with importance at the others, "without expressing... as in its last note... you understand... Besides, unless His Majesty the Emperor derogates from the principle of our alliance..."

"Wait, I have not finished..." he said to Prince Andrew, seizing him by the arm, "I believe that intervention will be stronger than nonintervention. And..." he paused. "Finally one cannot impute the nonreceipt of our dispatch of November 18. That is how it will end." And he released Bolkónski's arm to indicate that he had now quite finished.

"Demosthenes, I know thee by the pebble thou secretest in thy golden mouth!" said Bilíbin, and the mop of hair on his head moved with satisfaction.

Everybody laughed, and Hippolyte louder than anyone. He was evidently distressed, and breathed painfully, but could not restrain the wild laughter that convulsed his usually impassive features.

"Well now, gentlemen," said Bilíbin, "Bolkónski is my guest in this house and in Brünn itself. I want to entertain him as far as I can, with all the pleasures of life here. If we were in Vienna it would be easy, but here, in this wretched Moravian hole, it is more difficult, and I beg you all to help me. Brünn's attractions must be shown him. You can undertake the theater, I society, and you, Hippolyte, of course the women."

"We must let him see Amelie, she's exquisite!" said one of "ours," kissing his finger tips.

"In general we must turn this bloodthirsty soldier to more humane interests," said Bilíbin.

"I shall scarcely be able to avail myself of your hospitality, gentlemen, it is already time for me to go," replied Prince Andrew looking at his watch.

"Where to?"

"To the Emperor."

"Oh! Oh! Oh!"

"Well, *au revoir*, Bolkónski! *Au revoir*, Prince! Come back early to dinner," cried several voices. "We'll take you in hand."

"When speaking to the Emperor, try as far as you can to praise the way that provisions are supplied and the routes indicated," said Bilíbin, accompanying him to the hall.

"I should like to speak well of them, but as far as I know the facts, I can't," replied Bolkónski, smiling.

"Well, talk as much as you can, anyway. He has a passion for giving audiences, but he does not like talking himself and can't do it, as you will see."

CHAPTER XII

At the levee Prince Andrew stood among the Austrian officers as he had been told to, and the Emperor Francis merely looked fixedly into his face and just nodded to him with his long head. But after it was over, the adjutant he had seen the previous day ceremoniously informed Bolkónski that the Emperor desired to give him an audience. The Emperor Francis received him standing in the middle of the room. Before the conversation began Prince Andrew was struck by the fact that the Emperor seemed confused and blushed as if not knowing what to say.

"Tell me, when did the battle begin?" he asked hurriedly.

Prince Andrew replied. Then followed other questions just as simple: "Was Kutúzov well? When had he left Krems?" and so on. The Emperor spoke as if his sole aim were to put a given number of questions—the answers to these questions, as was only too evident, did not interest him.

"At what o'clock did the battle begin?" asked the Emperor.

"I cannot inform Your Majesty at what o'clock the battle began at the front, but at Dürrenstein, where I was, our attack began after five in the afternoon," replied Bolkónski growing more animated and expecting that he would have a chance to give a reliable account, which he had ready in his mind, of all he knew and had seen. But the Emperor smiled and interrupted him.

"How many miles?"

"From where to where, Your Majesty?"

"From Dürrenstein to Krems."

"Three and a half miles, Your Majesty."

"The French have abandoned the left bank?"

"According to the scouts the last of them crossed on rafts during the night."

"Is there sufficient forage in Krems?"

"Forage has not been supplied to the extent..."

The Emperor interrupted him.

"At what o'clock was General Schmidt killed?"

"At seven o'clock, I believe."

"At seven o'clock? It's very sad, very sad!"

The Emperor thanked Prince Andrew and bowed. Prince Andrew withdrew and was immediately surrounded by courtiers on all sides. Everywhere he saw friendly looks and heard friendly words. Yesterday's adjutant reproached him for not having stayed at the palace, and offered him his own house. The Minister of War came up and congratulated him on the Maria Theresa Order of the third grade, which the Emperor was conferring on him. The Empress' chamberlain invited him to see Her Majesty. The archduchess also wished to see him. He did not know whom to answer, and for a few seconds collected his thoughts. Then the Russian ambassador took him by the shoulder, led him to the window, and began to talk to him.

Contrary to Bilíbin's forecast the news he had brought was joyfully received. A thanksgiving service was arranged, Kutúzov was awarded the Grand Cross of Maria Theresa, and the whole army received rewards. Bolkónski was invited everywhere, and had to spend the whole morning calling on the principal Austrian dignitaries. Between four and five in the afternoon, having made all his calls, he was returning to Bilíbin's house thinking out a letter to his father about the battle and his visit to Brünn. At the door he found a vehicle half full of luggage. Franz, Bilíbin's man, was dragging a portmanteau with some difficulty out of the front door.

Before returning to Bilíbin's Prince Andrew had gone to a bookshop to provide himself with some books for the campaign, and had spent some time in the shop.

"What is it?" he asked.

"Oh, your excellency!" said Franz, with difficulty rolling the portmanteau into the vehicle, "we are to move on still farther. The scoundrel is again at our heels!"

"Eh? What?" asked Prince Andrew.

Bilíbin came out to meet him. His usually calm face showed excitement.

"There now! Confess that this is delightful," said he. "This affair of the Thabor Bridge, at Vienna.... They have crossed without striking a blow!"

Prince Andrew could not understand.

"But where do you come from not to know what every coachman in the town knows?"

"I come from the archduchess'. I heard nothing there."

"And you didn't see that everybody is packing up?"

"I did not... What is it all about?" inquired Prince Andrew impatiently.

"What's it all about? Why, the French have crossed the bridge that Auersperg was defending, and the bridge was not blown up: so Murat is now rushing along the road to Brünn and will be here in a day or two."

"What? Here? But why did they not blow up the bridge, if it was mined?"

"That is what I ask you. No one, not even Bonaparte, knows why."

Bolkónski shrugged his shoulders.

"But if the bridge is crossed it means that the army too is lost? It will be cut off," said he.

"That's just it," answered Bilíbin. "Listen! The French entered Vienna as I told you. Very well. Next day, which was yesterday, those gentlemen, *messieurs les maréchaux,* * Murat, Lannes, and Belliard, mount and ride to the bridge. (Observe that all three are Gascons.) 'Gentlemen,' says one of them, 'you know the Thabor Bridge is mined and doubly mined and that there are menacing fortifications at its head and an army of fifteen thousand men has been ordered to blow up the bridge and not let us cross? But it will please our sovereign the Emperor Napoleon if we take this bridge, so let us three go and take it!' 'Yes, let's!' say the others. And off they go and take the bridge, cross it, and now with their whole army are on this side of the Danube, marching on us, you, and your lines of communication."

* The marshalls.

"Stop jesting," said Prince Andrew sadly and seriously. This news grieved him and yet he was pleased.

As soon as he learned that the Russian army was in such a hopeless situation it occurred to him that it was he who was destined to lead it out of this position; that here was the Toulon that would lift him from the ranks of obscure officers and offer him the first step to fame! Listening to Bilíbin he was already imagining how on reaching the army he would give an opinion at the war council which would be the only one that could save the army, and how he alone would be entrusted with the executing of the plan.

"Stop this jesting," he said.

"I am not jesting," Bilíbin went on. "Nothing is truer or sadder. These gentlemen ride onto the bridge alone and wave white handkerchiefs; they assure the officer on duty that they, the marshals, are on their way to negotiate with Prince Auersperg. He lets them enter the *tête-de-pont.* * They spin him a thousand gasconades, saying that the war is over, that the Emperor Francis is arranging a meeting with Bonaparte, that they desire to see Prince Auersperg, and so on. The officer sends for Auersperg; these gentlemen embrace the officers, crack jokes, sit on the cannon, and meanwhile a French battalion gets to the bridge unobserved, flings the bags of incendiary material into the water, and approaches the *tête-de-pont.* At length appears the lieutenant general, our dear Prince Auersperg von Mautern himself. 'Dearest foe! Flower of the Austrian army, hero of the Turkish wars! Hostilities are ended, we can shake one another's hand.... The Emperor Napoleon burns with impatience to make Prince Auersperg's acquaintance.' In a word, those gentlemen, Gascons indeed, so bewildered him with fine words, and he is so flattered by his rapidly established intimacy with the French marshals, and so dazzled by the sight of Murat's mantle and ostrich plumes, *qu'iln'yvoit que du feu, et oublieceluiqu'ildevait faire faire sur l'ennemi!*' *(2) In spite of the animation of his speech, Bilíbin did not forget to pause after this mot to give time for its due appreciation. "The French battalion rushes to the bridgehead, spikes the guns, and the bridge is taken! But what is best of all," he went on, his excitement subsiding under the delightful interest of his own story, "is that the sergeant in charge of the cannon which was to give the signal to fire the mines and blow up the bridge, this sergeant, seeing that the French troops were running onto the bridge, was about to fire, but Lannes stayed his hand. The sergeant, who was evidently wiser than his general, goes up to Auersperg and says: 'Prince, you are being deceived, here are the French!' Murat, seeing that all is lost if the sergeant is allowed to speak, turns to Auersperg with feigned astonishment (he is a true Gascon) and says: 'I don't recognize the world-famous Austrian discipline, if you allow a subordinate to address you like that!' It was a stroke of genius. Prince Auersperg feels his dignity at stake and orders the sergeant to be arrested. Come, you must own that this affair of the Thabor Bridge is delightful! It is not exactly stupidity, nor rascality...."

* Bridgehead.

* (2) That their fire gets into his eyes and he forgets that he ought to be firing at the enemy.

"It may be treachery," said Prince Andrew, vividly imagining the gray overcoats, wounds, the smoke of gunpowder, the sounds of firing, and the glory that awaited him.

"Not that either. That puts the court in too bad a light," replied Bilíbin. "It's not treachery nor rascality nor stupidity: it is just as at Ulm... it is..."—he seemed to be trying to find the right expression. *"C'est... c'est du Mack. Nous sommesmackés* (It is... it is a bit of Mack. We are *Macked*)*," he concluded, feeling that he had produced a good epigram, a fresh one that would be repeated. His hitherto puckered brow became smooth as a sign of pleasure, and with a slight smile he began to examine his nails.

"Where are you off to?" he said suddenly to Prince Andrew who had risen and was going toward his room.

"I am going away."

"Where to?"

"To the army."

"But you meant to stay another two days?"

"But now I am off at once."

And Prince Andrew after giving directions about his departure went to his room.

"Do you know, *moncher*," said Bilíbin following him, "I have been thinking about you. Why are you going?"

And in proof of the conclusiveness of his opinion all the wrinkles vanished from his face.

Prince Andrew looked inquiringly at him and gave no reply.

"Why are you going? I know you think it your duty to gallop back to the army now that it is in danger. I understand that. *Mon cher*, it is heroism!"

"Not at all," said Prince Andrew.

"But as you are a philosopher, be a consistent one, look at the other side of the question and you will see that your duty, on the contrary, is to take care of yourself. Leave it to those who are no longer fit for anything else.... You have not been ordered to return and have not been dismissed from here; therefore, you can stay and go with us wherever our ill luck takes us. They say we are going to Olmütz, and Olmütz is a very decent town. You and I will travel comfortably in my *calèche*."

"Do stop joking, Bilíbin," cried Bolkónski.

"I am speaking sincerely as a friend! Consider! Where and why are you going, when you might remain here? You are faced by one of two things," and the skin over his left temple puckered, "either you will not reach your regiment before peace is concluded, or you will share defeat and disgrace with Kutúzov's whole army."

And Bilíbin unwrinkled his temple, feeling that the dilemma was insoluble.

"I cannot argue about it," replied Prince Andrew coldly, but he thought: "I am going to save the army."

"My dear fellow, you are a hero!" said Bilíbin.

CHAPTER XIII

That same night, having taken leave of the Minister of War, Bolkónski set off to rejoin the army, not knowing where he would find it and fearing to be captured by the French on the way to Krems.

In Brünn everybody attached to the court was packing up, and the heavy baggage was already being dispatched to Olmütz. Near Hetzelsdorf Prince Andrew struck the high road along which the Russian army was moving with great haste and in the greatest disorder. The road was so obstructed with carts that it was impossible to get by in a carriage. Prince Andrew took a horse and a Cossack from a Cossack commander, and hungry and weary, making his way past the baggage wagons, rode in search of the commander in chief and of his own luggage. Very sinister reports of the position of the army reached him as he went along, and the appearance of the troops in their disorderly flight confirmed these rumors.

"Cettearmée russe que l'or de l'Angleterre a transportée des extrémités de l'univers, nous allonslui faire éprouver le même sort—(le sort de l'arméed'Ulm)." * He remembered these words in Bonaparte's address to his army at the beginning of the campaign, and they awoke in him astonishment at the genius of his hero, a feeling of wounded pride, and a hope of glory. "And should there be nothing left but to die?" he thought. "Well, if need be, I shall do it no worse than others."

* "That Russian army which has been brought from the ends of the earth by English gold, we shall cause to share the same fate—(the fate of the army at Ulm)."

He looked with disdain at the endless confused mass of detachments, carts, guns, artillery, and again baggage wagons and vehicles of all kinds overtaking one another and blocking the muddy road, three and sometimes four abreast. From all sides, behind and before, as far as ear could reach, there were the rattle of wheels, the creaking of carts and gun carriages, the tramp of horses, the crack of whips, shouts, the urging of horses, and the swearing of soldiers, orderlies, and officers. All along the sides of the road fallen horses were to be seen, some flayed, some not, and broken-down carts beside which solitary soldiers sat waiting for something, and again soldiers straggling from their companies, crowds of whom set off to the neighboringvillages, or returned from them dragging sheep, fowls, hay, and bulging sacks. At each ascent or descent of the road the crowds were yet denser and the din of shouting more incessant. Soldiers floundering knee-deep in mud pushed the guns and wagons themselves. Whips cracked, hoofs slipped, traces broke, and lungs were strained with shouting. The officers directing the march rode backward and forward between the carts. Their voices were but feebly heard amid the uproar and one saw by their faces that they despaired of the possibility of checking this disorder.

"Here is our dear Orthodox Russian army," thought Bolkónski, recalling Bilíbin's words.

Wishing to find out where the commander in chief was, he rode up to a convoy. Directly opposite to him came a strange one-horse vehicle, evidently rigged up by soldiers out of any available materials and looking like something between a cart, a cabriolet, and a *calèche*. A soldier was driving, and a woman enveloped in shawls sat behind the apron under the leather hood of the vehicle. Prince Andrew rode up and was just putting his question to a soldier when his attention was diverted by the desperate shrieks of the woman in the vehicle. An officer in charge of transport was beating the soldier who was driving the woman's vehicle for trying to get ahead of others, and the strokes of his whip fell on the apron of the equipage. The woman screamed piercingly. Seeing Prince Andrew she leaned out from behind the apron and, waving her thin arms from under the woolen shawl, cried:

"Mr. Aide-de-camp! Mr. Aide-de-camp!... For heaven's sake... Protect me! What will become of us? I am the wife of the doctor of the Seventh Chasseurs.... They won't let us pass, we are left behind and have lost our people..."

"I'll flatten you into a pancake!" shouted the angry officer to the soldier. "Turn back with your slut!"

"Mr. Aide-de-camp! Help me!... What does it all mean?" screamed the doctor's wife.

"Kindly let this cart pass. Don't you see it's a woman?" said Prince Andrew riding up to the officer.

The officer glanced at him, and without replying turned again to the soldier. "I'll teach you to push on!... Back!"

"Let them pass, I tell you!" repeated Prince Andrew, compressing his lips.

"And who are you?" cried the officer, turning on him with tipsy rage, "who are *you?* Are you in command here? Eh? I am commander here, not you! Go back or I'll flatten you into a pancake," repeated he. This expression evidently pleased him.

"That was a nice snub for the little aide-de-camp," came a voice from behind.

Prince Andrew saw that the officer was in that state of senseless, tipsy rage when a man does not know what he is saying. He saw that his championship of the doctor's wife in her queer trap might expose him to what he dreaded more than anything in the world—to ridicule; but his instinct urged him on. Before the officer finished his sentence Prince Andrew, his face distorted with fury, rode up to him and raised his riding whip.

"Kind...ly let—them—pass!"

The officer flourished his arm and hastily rode away.

"It's all the fault of these fellows on the staff that there's this disorder," he muttered. "Do as you like."

Prince Andrew without lifting his eyes rode hastily away from the doctor's wife, who was calling him her deliverer, and recalling with a sense of disgust the minutest details of this humiliating scene he galloped on to the village where he was told who the commander in chief was.

On reaching the village he dismounted and went to the nearest house, intending to rest if but for a moment, eat something, and try to sort out the stinging and tormenting thoughts that confused his mind. "This is a mob of scoundrels and not an army," he was thinking as he went up to the window of the first house, when a familiar voice called him by name.

He turned round. Nesvítski's handsome face looked out of the little window. Nesvítski, moving his moist lips as he chewed something, and flourishing his arm, called him to enter.

"Bolkónski! Bolkónski!... Don't you hear? Eh? Come quick..." he shouted.

Entering the house, Prince Andrew saw Nesvítski and another adjutant having something to eat. They hastily turned round to him asking if he had any news. On their familiar faces he read agitation and alarm. This was particularly noticeable on Nesvítski's usually laughing countenance.

"Where is the commander in chief?" asked Bolkónski.

"Here, in that house," answered the adjutant.

"Well, is it true that it's peace and capitulation?" asked Nesvítski.

"I was going to ask you. I know nothing except that it was all I could do to get here."

"And we, my dear boy! It's terrible! I was wrong to laugh at Mack, we're getting it still worse," said Nesvítski. "But sit down and have something to eat."

"You won't be able to find either your baggage or anything else now, Prince. And God only knows where your man Peter is," said the other adjutant.

"Where are headquarters?"

"We are to spend the night in Znaim."

"Well, I have got all I need into packs for two horses," said Nesvítski. "They've made up splendid packs for me—fit to cross the Bohemian mountains with. It's a bad lookout, old fellow! But what's the matter with you? You must be ill to shiver like that," he added, noticing that Prince Andrew winced as at an electric shock.

"It's nothing," replied Prince Andrew.

He had just remembered his recent encounter with the doctor's wife and the convoy officer.

"What is the commander in chief doing here?" he asked.

"I can't make out at all," said Nesvítski.

"Well, all I can make out is that everything is abominable, abominable, quite abominable!" said Prince Andrew, and he went off to the house where the commander in chief was.

Passing by Kutúzov's carriage and the exhausted saddle horses of his suite, with their Cossacks who were talking loudly together, Prince Andrew entered the passage. Kutúzov himself, he was told, was in the house with Prince Bagratión and Weyrother. Weyrother was the Austrian general who had succeeded Schmidt. In the passage little Kozlóvski was squatting on his heels in front of a clerk. The clerk, with cuffs turned up, was hastily writing at a tub turned bottom upwards. Kozlóvski's face looked worn—he too had evidently not slept all night. He glanced at Prince Andrew and did not even nod to him.

"Second line... have you written it?" he continued dictating to the clerk. "The Kiev Grenadiers, Podolian..."

"One can't write so fast, your honor," said the clerk, glancing angrily and disrespectfully at Kozlóvski.

Through the door came the sounds of Kutúzov's voice, excited and dissatisfied, interrupted by another, an unfamiliar voice. From the sound of these voices, the inattentive way Kozlóvski looked at him, the disrespectful manner of the exhausted clerk, the fact that the clerk and Kozlóvski were squatting on the floor by a tub so near to the commander in chief, and from the noisy laughter of the Cossacks holding the horses near the window, Prince Andrew felt that something important and disastrous was about to happen.

He turned to Kozlóvski with urgent questions.

"Immediately, Prince," said Kozlóvski. "Dispositions for Bagratión."

"What about capitulation?"

"Nothing of the sort. Orders are issued for a battle."

Prince Andrew moved toward the door from whence voices were heard. Just as he was going to open it the sounds ceased, the door opened, and Kutúzov with his eagle nose and puffy face appeared in the doorway. Prince Andrew stood right in front of Kutúzov but the expression of the commander in chief's one sound eye showed him to be so preoccupied with thoughts and anxieties as to be oblivious of his presence. He looked straight at his adjutant's face without recognizing him.

"Well, have you finished?" said he to Kozlóvski.

"One moment, your excellency."

Bagratión, a gaunt middle-aged man of medium height with a firm, impassive face of Oriental type, came out after the commander in chief.

"I have the honor to present myself," repeated Prince Andrew rather loudly, handing Kutúzov an envelope.

"Ah, from Vienna? Very good. Later, later!"

Kutúzov went out into the porch with Bagratión.

"Well, good-by, Prince," said he to Bagratión. "My blessing, and may Christ be with you in your great endeavor!"

His face suddenly softened and tears came into his eyes. With his left hand he drew Bagratión toward him, and with his right, on which he wore a ring, he made the sign of the cross over him with a gesture evidently habitual, offering his puffy cheek, but Bagratión kissed him on the neck instead.

"Christ be with you!" Kutúzov repeated and went toward his carriage. "Get in with me," said he to Bolkónski.

"Your excellency, I should like to be of use here. Allow me to remain with Prince Bagratión's detachment."

"Get in," said Kutúzov, and noticing that Bolkónski still delayed, he added: "I need good officers myself, need them myself!"

They got into the carriage and drove for a few minutes in silence.

"There is still much, much before us," he said, as if with an old man's penetration he understood all that was passing in Bolkónski's mind. "If a tenth part of his detachment returns I shall thank God," he added as if speaking to himself.

Prince Andrew glanced at Kutúzov's face only a foot distant from him and involuntarily noticed the carefully washed seams of the scar near his temple, where an Ismail bullet had pierced his skull, and the empty eye socket. "Yes, he has a right to speak so calmly of those men's death," thought Bolkónski.

"That is why I beg to be sent to that detachment," he said.

Kutúzov did not reply. He seemed to have forgotten what he had been saying, and sat plunged in thought. Five minutes later, gently swaying on the soft springs of the carriage, he turned to Prince Andrew. There was not a trace of agitation on his face. With delicate irony he questioned Prince Andrew about the details of his interview with the Emperor, about the remarks he had heard at court concerning the Krems affair, and about some ladies they both knew.

CHAPTER XIV

O n November 1 Kutúzov had received, through a spy, news that the army he commanded was in an almost hopeless position. The spy reported that the French, after crossing the bridge at Vienna, were advancing in immense force upon Kutúzov's line of communication with the troops that were arriving from Russia. If Kutúzov decided to remain at Krems, Napoleon's army of one hundred and fifty thousand men would cut him off completely and surround his exhausted army of forty thousand, and he would find himself in the position of Mack at Ulm. If Kutúzov decided to abandon the road connecting him with the troops arriving from Russia, he would have to march with no road into unknown parts of the Bohemian mountains, defending himself against superior forces of the enemy and abandoning all hope of a junction with Buxhöwden. If Kutúzov decided to retreat along the road from Krems to Olmütz, to unite with the troops arriving from Russia, he risked being forestalled on that road by the French who had crossed the Vienna bridge, and encumbered by his baggage and transport, having to accept battle on the march against an enemy three times as strong, who would hem him in from two sides.

Kutúzov chose this latter course.

The French, the spy reported, having crossed the Vienna bridge, were advancing by forced marches toward Znaim, which lay sixty-six miles off on the line of Kutúzov's retreat. If he reached Znaim before the French, there would be great hope of saving the army; to let the French forestall him at Znaim meant the exposure of his whole army to a disgrace such as that of Ulm, or to utter destruction. But to forestall the French with his whole army was impossible. The road for the French from Vienna to Znaim was shorter and better than the road for the Russians from Krems to Znaim.

The night he received the news, Kutúzov sent Bagratión's vanguard, four thousand strong, to the right across the hills from the Krems-Znaim to the Vienna-Znaim road. Bagratión was to make this march without resting, and to halt facing Vienna with Znaim to his rear, and if he succeeded in forestalling the French he was to delay them as long as possible. Kutúzov himself with all his transport took the road to Znaim.

Marching thirty miles that stormy night across roadless hills, with his hungry, ill-shod soldiers, and losing a third of his men as stragglers by the way, Bagratión came out on the Vienna-Znaim road at Hollabrünn a few hours ahead of the French who were approaching Hollabrünn from Vienna. Kutúzov with his transport had still to march for some days before he could reach Znaim. Hence Bagratión with his four thousand hungry, exhausted men would have to detain for days the whole enemy army that came upon him at Hollabrünn, which was clearly impossible. But a freak of fate made the impossible possible. The success of the trick that had placed the Vienna bridge in the hands of the French without a fight led Murat to try to deceive Kutúzov in a similar way. Meeting Bagratión's weak detachment on the Znaim road he supposed it to be Kutúzov's whole army. To be able to crush it absolutely he awaited the arrival of the rest of the troops who were on their way from Vienna, and with this object offered a three days' truce on condition that both armies should remain in position without moving. Murat declared that negotiations for peace were already proceeding, and that he therefore offered this truce to avoid unnecessary bloodshed. Count Nostitz, the Austrian general occupying the advanced posts, believed Murat's emissary and retired, leaving Bagratión's division exposed. Another emissary rode to the Russian line to announce the peace negotiations and to offer the Russian army the three days' truce. Bagratión replied that he was not authorized either to accept or refuse a truce and sent his adjutant to Kutúzov to report the offer he had received.

A truce was Kutúzov's sole chance of gaining time, giving Bagratión's exhausted troops some rest, and letting the transport and heavy convoys (whose movements were concealed from the French) advance if but one stage nearer Znaim. The offer of a truce gave the only, and a quite unexpected, chance of saving the army. On receiving the news he immediately dispatched Adjutant General Wintzingerode, who was in attendance on him, to the enemy camp.

Wintzingerode was not merely to agree to the truce but also to offer terms of capitulation, and meanwhile Kutúzov sent his adjutants back to hasten to the utmost the movements of the baggage trains of the entire army along the Krems-Znaim road. Bagratión's exhausted and hungry detachment, which alone covered this movement of the transport and of the whole army, had to remain stationary in face of an enemy eight times as strong as itself.

Kutúzov's expectations that the proposals of capitulation (which were in no way binding) might give time for part of the transport to pass, and also that Murat's mistake would very soon be discovered, proved correct. As soon as Bonaparte (who was at Schönbrunn, sixteen miles from Hollabrünn) received Murat's dispatch with the proposal of a truce and a capitulation, he detected a ruse and wrote the following letter to Murat:

Schönbrunn, 25th Brumaire, 1805,

at eight o'clock in the morning

To PRINCE MURAT,

I cannot find words to express to you my displeasure. You command only my advance guard, and have no right to arrange an armistice without my order. You are causing me to lose the fruits of a campaign. Break the armistice immediately and march on the enemy. Inform him that the general who signed that capitulation had no right to do so, and that no one but the Emperor of Russia has that right.

If, however, the Emperor of Russia ratifies that convention, I will ratify it; but it is only a trick. March on, destroy the Russian army.... You are in a position to seize its baggage and artillery.

The Russian Emperor's aide-de-camp is an impostor. Officers are nothing when they have no powers; this one had none.... The Austrians let themselves be tricked at the crossing of the Vienna bridge, you are letting yourself be tricked by an aide-de-camp of the Emperor.

NAPOLEON

Bonaparte's adjutant rode full gallop with this menacing letter to Murat. Bonaparte himself, not trusting to his generals, moved with all the Guards to the field of battle, afraid of letting a ready victim escape, and Bagratión's four thousand men merrily lighted campfires, dried and warmed themselves, cooked their porridge for the first time for three days, and not one of them knew or imagined what was in store for him.

CHAPTER XV

Between three and four o'clock in the afternoon Prince Andrew, who had persisted in his request to Kutúzov, arrived at Grunth and reported himself to Bagratión. Bonaparte's adjutant had not yet reached Murat's detachment and the battle had not yet begun. In Bagratión's detachment no one knew anything of the general position of affairs. They talked of peace but did not believe in its possibility; others talked of a battle but also disbelieved in the nearness of an engagement. Bagratión, knowing Bolkónski to be a favorite and trusted adjutant, received him with distinction and special marks of favor, explaining to him that there would probably be an engagement that day or the next, and giving him full liberty to remain with him during the battle or to join the rearguard and have an eye on the order of retreat, "which is also very important."

"However, there will hardly be an engagement today," said Bagratión as if to reassure Prince Andrew.

"If he is one of the ordinary little staff dandies sent to earn a medal he can get his reward just as well in the rearguard, but if he wishes to stay with me, let him... he'll be of use here if he's a brave officer," thought Bagratión. Prince Andrew, without replying, asked the prince's permission to ride round the position to see the disposition of the forces, so as to know his bearings should he be sent to execute an order. The officer on duty, a handsome, elegantly dressed man with a diamond ring on his forefinger, who was fond of speaking French though he spoke it badly, offered to conduct Prince Andrew.

On all sides they saw rain-soaked officers with dejected faces who seemed to be seeking something, and soldiers dragging doors, benches, and fencing from the village.

"There now, Prince! We can't stop those fellows," said the staff officer pointing to the soldiers. "The officers don't keep them in hand. And there," he pointed to a sutler's tent, "they crowd in and sit. This morning I turned them all out and now look, it's full again. I must go there, Prince, and scare them a bit. It won't take a moment."

"Yes, let's go in and I will get myself a roll and some cheese," said Prince Andrew who had not yet had time to eat anything.

"Why didn't you mention it, Prince? I would have offered you something."

They dismounted and entered the tent. Several officers, with flushed and weary faces, were sitting at the table eating and drinking.

"Now what does this mean, gentlemen?" said the staff officer, in the reproachful tone of a man who has repeated the same thing more than once. "You know it won't do to leave your posts like this. The prince gave orders that no one should leave his post. Now you, Captain," and he turned to a thin, dirty little artillery officer who without his boots (he had given them to the canteen keeper to dry), in only his stockings, rose when they entered, smiling not altogether comfortably.

"Well, aren't you ashamed of yourself, Captain Túshin?" he continued. "One would think that as an artillery officer you would set a good example, yet here you are without your boots! The alarm will be sounded and you'll be in a pretty position without your boots!" (The staff officer smiled.) "Kindly return to your posts, gentlemen, all of you, all!" he added in a tone of command.

Prince Andrew smiled involuntarily as he looked at the artillery officer Túshin, who silent and smiling, shifting from one stockinged foot to the other, glanced inquiringly with his large, intelligent, kindly eyes from Prince Andrew to the staff officer.

"The soldiers say it feels easier without boots," said Captain Túshin smiling shyly in his uncomfortable position, evidently wishing to adopt a jocular tone. But before he had finished he felt that his jest was unacceptable and had not come off. He grew confused.

"Kindly return to your posts," said the staff officer trying to preserve his gravity.

Prince Andrew glanced again at the artillery officer's small figure. There was something peculiar about it, quite unsoldierly, rather comic, but extremely attractive.

The staff officer and Prince Andrew mounted their horses and rode on.

Having ridden beyond the village, continually meeting and overtaking soldiers and officers of various regiments, they saw on their left some entrenchments being thrown up, the freshly dug clay of which showed up red. Several battalions of soldiers, in their shirt sleeves despite the cold wind, swarmed in these earthworks like a host of white ants; spadefuls of red clay were continually being thrown up from behind the bank by unseen hands. Prince Andrew and the officer rode up, looked at the entrenchment, and went on again. Just behind it they came upon some dozens of soldiers, continually replaced by others, who ran from the entrenchment. They had to hold their noses and put their horses to a trot to escape from the poisoned atmosphere of these latrines.

"Voilà l'agrément des camps, monsieur le prince," * said the staff officer.

* "This is a pleasure one gets in camp, Prince."

They rode up the opposite hill. From there the French could already be seen. Prince Andrew stopped and began examining the position.

"That's our battery," said the staff officer indicating the highest point. "It's in charge of the queer fellow we saw without his boots. You can see everything from there; let's go there, Prince."

"Thank you very much, I will go on alone," said Prince Andrew, wishing to rid himself of this staff officer's company, "please don't trouble yourself further."

The staff officer remained behind and Prince Andrew rode on alone.

The farther forward and nearer the enemy he went, the more orderly and cheerful were the troops. The greatest disorder and depression had been in the baggage train he had passed that morning on the Znaim road seven miles away from the French. At Grunth also some apprehension and alarm could be felt, but the nearer Prince Andrew came to the French lines the more confident was the appearance of our troops. The soldiers in their greatcoats were ranged in lines, the sergeants major and company officers were counting the men, poking the last man in each section in the ribs and telling him to hold his hand up. Soldiers scattered over the whole place were dragging logs and brushwood and were building shelters with merry chatter and laughter; around the fires sat others, dressed and undressed, drying their shirts and leg bands or mending boots or overcoats and crowding round the boilers and porridge cookers. In one company dinner was ready, and the soldiers were gazing eagerly at the steaming boiler, waiting till the sample, which a quartermaster sergeant was carrying in a wooden bowl to an officer who sat on a log before his shelter, had been tasted.

Another company, a lucky one for not all the companies had vodka, crowded round a pockmarked, broad-shouldered sergeant major who, tilting a keg, filled one after another the canteen lids held out to him. The soldiers lifted the canteen lids to their lips with reverential faces, emptied them, rolling the vodka in their mouths, and walked away from the sergeant major with brightened expressions, licking their lips and wiping them on the sleeves of their greatcoats. All their faces were as serene as if all this were happening at home awaiting peaceful encampment, and not within sight of the enemy before an action in which at least half of them would be left on the field. After passing a chasseur regiment and in the lines of the Kiev grenadiers—fine fellows busy with similar peaceful affairs—near the shelter of the regimental commander, higher than and different from the others, Prince Andrew came out in front of a platoon of grenadiers before whom lay a naked man. Two soldiers held him while two others were flourishing their switches and striking him regularly on his bare back. The man shrieked unnaturally. A stout major was pacing up and down the line, and regardless of the screams kept repeating:

"It's a shame for a soldier to steal; a soldier must be honest, honorable, and brave, but if he robs his fellows there is no honor in him, he's a scoundrel. Go on! Go on!"

So the swishing sound of the strokes, and the desperate but unnatural screams, continued.

"Go on, go on!" said the major.

A young officer with a bewildered and pained expression on his face stepped away from the man and looked round inquiringly at the adjutant as he rode by.

Prince Andrew, having reached the front line, rode along it. Our front line and that of the enemy were far apart on the right and left flanks, but in the center where the men with a flag of truce had passed that morning, the lines were so near together that the men could see one another's faces and speak to one another. Besides the soldiers who formed the picket line on either side, there were many curious onlookers who, jesting and laughing, stared at their strange foreign enemies.

Since early morning—despite an injunction not to approach the picket line—the officers had been unable to keep sight-seers away. The soldiers forming the picket line, like showmen exhibiting a curiosity, no longer looked at the French but paid attention to the sight-seers and grew weary waiting to be relieved. Prince Andrew halted to have a look at the French.

"Look! Look there!" one soldier was saying to another, pointing to a Russian musketeer who had gone up to the picket line with an officer and was rapidly and excitedly talking to a French grenadier. "Hark to him jabbering! Fine, isn't it? It's all the Frenchy can do to keep up with him. There now, Sídorov!"

"Wait a bit and listen. It's fine!" answered Sídorov, who was considered an adept at French.

The soldier to whom the laughers referred was Dólokhov. Prince Andrew recognized him and stopped to listen to what he was saying. Dólokhov had come from the left flank where their regiment was stationed, with his captain.

"Now then, go on, go on!" incited the officer, bending forward and trying not to lose a word of the speech which was incomprehensible to him. "More, please: more! What's he saying?"

Dólokhov did not answer the captain; he had been drawn into a hot dispute with the French grenadier. They were naturally talking about the campaign. The Frenchman, confusing the Austrians with the Russians, was trying to prove that the Russians had surrendered and had fled all the way from Ulm, while Dólokhov maintained that the Russians had not surrendered but had beaten the French.

"We have orders to drive you off here, and we shall drive you off," said Dólokhov.

"Only take care you and your Cossacks are not all captured!" said the French grenadier.

The French onlookers and listeners laughed.

"We'll make you dance as we did under Suvórov...," * said Dólokhov.

* "On vousferadanser."

"Qu' est-cequ'ilchante?" * asked a Frenchman.

* "What's he singing about?"

"It's ancient history," said another, guessing that it referred to a former war. "The Emperor will teach your Suvara as he has taught the others..."

"Bonaparte..." began Dólokhov, but the Frenchman interrupted him.

"Not Bonaparte. He is the Emperor! *Sacré nom...!*" cried he angrily.

"The devil skin your Emperor."

And Dólokhov swore at him in coarse soldier's Russian and shouldering his musket walked away.

"Let us go, Iván Lukích," he said to the captain.

"Ah, that's the way to talk French," said the picket soldiers. "Now, Sídorov, you have a try!"

Sídorov, turning to the French, winked, and began to jabber meaningless sounds very fast: *"Kari, mala, tafa, safi, muter, Kaská,"* he said, trying to give an expressive intonation to his voice.

"Ho! ho! ho! Ha! ha! ha! ha! Ouh! ouh!" came peals of such healthy and good-humored laughter from the soldiers that it infected the French involuntarily, so much so that the only thing left to do seemed to be to unload the muskets, explode the ammunition, and all return home as quickly as possible.

But the guns remained loaded, the loopholes in blockhouses and entrenchments looked out just as menacingly, and the unlimbered cannon confronted one another as before.

CHAPTER XVI

Having ridden round the whole line from right flank to left, Prince Andrew made his way up to the battery from which the staff officer had told him the whole field could be seen. Here he dismounted, and stopped beside the farthest of the four unlimbered cannon. Before the guns an artillery sentry was pacing up and down; he stood at attention when the officer arrived, but at a sign resumed his measured, monotonous pacing. Behind the guns were their limbers and still farther back picket ropes and artillerymen's bonfires. To the left, not far from the farthest cannon, was a small, newly constructed wattle shed from which came the sound of officers' voices in eager conversation.

It was true that a view over nearly the whole Russian position and the greater part of the enemy's opened out from this battery. Just facing it, on the crest of the opposite hill, the village of Schön Grabern could be seen, and in three places to left and right the French troops amid the smoke of their campfires, the greater part of whom were evidently in the village itself and behind the hill. To the left from that village, amid the smoke, was something resembling a battery, but it was impossible to see it clearly with the naked eye. Our right flank was posted on a rather steep incline which dominated the French position. Our infantry were stationed there, and at the farthest point the dragoons. In the center, where Túshin's battery stood and from which Prince Andrew was surveying the position, was the easiest and most direct descent and ascent to the brook separating us from Schön Grabern. On the left our troops were close to a copse, in which smoked the bonfires of our infantry who were felling wood. The French line was wider than ours, and it was plain that they could easily outflank us on both sides. Behind our position was a steep and deep dip, making it difficult for artillery and cavalry to retire. Prince Andrew took out his notebook and, leaning on the cannon, sketched a plan of the position. He made some notes on two points, intending to mention them to Bagratión. His idea was, first, to concentrate all the artillery in the center, and secondly, to withdraw the cavalry to the other side of the dip. Prince Andrew, being always near the commander in chief, closely following the mass movements and general orders, and constantly studying historical accounts of battles, involuntarily pictured to himself the course of events in the forthcoming action in broad outline. He imagined only important possibilities: "If the enemy attacks the right flank," he said to himself, "the Kiev grenadiers and the Podólsk chasseurs must hold their position till reserves from the center come up. In that case the dragoons could successfully make a flank counterattack. If they attack our center we, having the center battery on this high ground, shall withdraw the left flank under its cover, and retreat to the dip by echelons." So he reasoned.... All the time he had been beside the gun, he had heard the voices of the officers distinctly, but as often happens had not understood a word of what they were saying. Suddenly, however, he was struck by a voice coming from the shed, and its tone was so sincere that he could not but listen.

"No, friend," said a pleasant and, as it seemed to Prince Andrew, a familiar voice, "what I say is that if it were possible to know what is beyond death, none of us would be afraid of it. That's so, friend."

Another, a younger voice, interrupted him: "Afraid or not, you can't escape it anyhow."

"All the same, one is afraid! Oh, you clever people," said a third manly voice interrupting them both. "Of course you artillery men are very wise, because you can take everything along with you—vodka and snacks."

And the owner of the manly voice, evidently an infantry officer, laughed.

"Yes, one is afraid," continued the first speaker, he of the familiar voice. "One is afraid of the unknown, that's what it is. Whatever we may say about the soul going to the sky... we know there is no sky but only an atmosphere."

The manly voice again interrupted the artillery officer.

"Well, stand us some of your herb vodka, Túshin," it said.

"Why," thought Prince Andrew, "that's the captain who stood up in the sutler's hut without his boots." He recognized the agreeable, philosophizing voice with pleasure.

"Some herb vodka? Certainly!" said Túshin. "But still, to conceive a future life..."

He did not finish. Just then there was a whistle in the air; nearer and nearer, faster and louder, louder and faster, a cannon ball, as if it had not finished saying what was necessary, thudded into the ground near the shed with super human force, throwing up a mass of earth. The ground seemed to groan at the terrible impact.

And immediately Túshin, with a short pipe in the corner of his mouth and his kind, intelligent face rather pale, rushed out of the shed followed by the owner of the manly voice, a dashing infantry officer who hurried off to his company, buttoning up his coat as he ran.

CHAPTER XVII

Mounting his horse again Prince Andrew lingered with the battery, looking at the puff from the gun that had sent the ball. His eyes ran rapidly over the wide space, but he only saw that the hitherto motionless masses of the French now swayed and that there really was a battery to their left. The smoke above it had not yet dispersed. Two mounted Frenchmen, probably adjutants, were galloping up the hill. A small but distinctly visible enemy column was moving down the hill, probably to strengthen the front line. The smoke of the first shot had not yet dispersed before another puff appeared, followed by a report. The battle had begun! Prince Andrew turned his horse and galloped back to Grunth to find Prince Bagratión. He heard the cannonade behind him growing louder and more frequent. Evidently our guns had begun to reply. From the bottom of the slope, where the parleys had taken place, came the report of musketry.

Lemarrois had just arrived at a gallop with Bonaparte's stern letter, and Murat, humiliated and anxious to expiate his fault, had at once moved his forces to attack the center and outflank both the Russian wings, hoping before evening and before the arrival of the Emperorto crush the contemptible detachment that stood before him.

"It has begun. Here it is!" thought Prince Andrew, feeling the blood rush to his heart. "But where and how will my Toulon present itself?"

Passing between the companies that had been eating porridge and drinking vodka a quarter of an hour before, he saw everywhere the same rapid movement of soldiers forming ranks and getting their muskets ready, and on all their faces he recognized the same eagerness that filled his heart. "It has begun! Here it is, dreadful but enjoyable!" was what the face of each soldier and each officer seemed to say.

Before he had reached the embankments that were being thrown up, he saw, in the light of the dull autumn evening, mounted men coming toward him. The foremost, wearing a Cossack cloak and lambskin cap and riding a white horse, was Prince Bagratión. Prince Andrew stopped, waiting for him to come up; Prince Bagratión reined in his horse and recognizing Prince Andrew nodded to him. He still looked ahead while Prince Andrew told him what he had seen.

The feeling, "It has begun! Here it is!" was seen even on Prince Bagratión's hard brown face with its half-closed, dull, sleepy eyes. Prince Andrew gazed with anxious curiosity at that impassive face and wished he could tell what, if anything, this man was thinking and feeling at that moment. "Is there anything at all behind that impassive face?" Prince Andrew asked himself as he looked. Prince Bagratión bent his head in sign of agreement with what Prince Andrew told him, and said, "Very good!" in a tone that seemed to imply that everything that took place and was reported to him was exactly what he had foreseen. Prince Andrew, out of breath with his rapid ride, spoke quickly. Prince Bagratión, uttering his words with an Oriental accent, spoke particularly slowly, as if to impress the fact that there was no need to hurry. However, he put his horse to a trot in the direction of Túshin's battery. Prince Andrew followed with the suite. Behind Prince Bagratión rode an officer of the suite, the prince's personal adjutant, Zherkóv, an orderly officer, the staff officer on duty, riding a fine bobtailed horse, and a civilian—an accountant who had asked permission to be present at the battle out of curiosity. The accountant, a stout, full-faced man, looked around him with a naïve smile of satisfaction and presented a strange appearance among the hussars, Cossacks, and adjutants, in his camlet coat, as he jolted on his horse with a convoy officer's saddle.

"He wants to see a battle," said Zherkóv to Bolkónski, pointing to the accountant, "but he feels a pain in the pit of his stomach already."

"Oh, leave off!" said the accountant with a beaming but rather cunning smile, as if flattered at being made the subject of Zherkóv's joke, and purposely trying to appear stupider than he really was.

"It is very strange, *mon Monsieur Prince*," said the staff officer. (He remembered that in French there is some peculiar way of addressing a prince, but could not get it quite right.)

By this time they were all approaching Túshin's battery, and a ball struck the ground in front of them.

"What's that that has fallen?" asked the accountant with a naïve smile.

"A French pancake," answered Zherkóv.

"So that's what they hit with?" asked the accountant. "How awful!"

He seemed to swell with satisfaction. He had hardly finished speaking when they again heard an unexpectedly violent whistling which suddenly ended with a thud into something soft... *f-f-flop!* and a Cossack, riding a little to their right and behind the accountant, crashed to earth with his horse. Zherkóv and the staff officer bent over their saddles and turned their horses away. The accountant stopped, facing the Cossack, and examined him with attentive curiosity. The Cossack was dead, but the horse still struggled.

Prince Bagratión screwed up his eyes, looked round, and, seeing the cause of the confusion, turned away with indifference, as if to say, "Is it worth while noticing trifles?" He reined in his horse with the care of a skillful rider and, slightly bending over, disengaged his saber which had caught in his cloak. It was an old-fashioned saber of a kind no longer in general use. Prince Andrew remembered the story of Suvórov giving his saber to Bagratión in Italy, and the recollection was particularly pleasant at that moment. They had reached the battery at which Prince Andrew had been when he examined the battlefield.

"Whose company?" asked Prince Bagratión of an artilleryman standing by the ammunition wagon.

He asked, "Whose company?" but he really meant, "Are you frightened here?" and the artilleryman understood him.

"Captain Túshin's, your excellency!" shouted the red-haired, freckled gunner in a merry voice, standing to attention.

"Yes, yes," muttered Bagratión as if considering something, and he rode past the limbers to the farthest cannon.

As he approached, a ringing shot issued from it deafening him and his suite, and in the smoke that suddenly surrounded the gun they could see the gunners who had seized it straining to roll it quickly back to its former position. A huge, broad-shouldered gunner, Number One, holding a mop, his legs far apart, sprang to the wheel; while Number Two with a trembling hand placed a charge in the cannon's mouth. The short, round-shouldered Captain Túshin, stumbling over the tail of the gun carriage, moved forward and, not noticing the general, looked out shading his eyes with his small hand.

"Lift it two lines more and it will be just right," cried he in a feeble voice to which he tried to impart a dashing note, ill-suited to his weak figure. "Number Two!" he squeaked. "Fire, Medvédev!"

Bagratión called to him, and Túshin, raising three fingers to his cap with a bashful and awkward gesture not at all like a military salute but like a priest's benediction, approached the general. Though Túshin's guns had been intended to cannonade the valley, he was firing incendiary balls at the village of Schön Grabern visible just opposite, in front of which large masses of French were advancing.

No one had given Túshin orders where and at what to fire, but after consulting his sergeant major, Zakharchénko, for whom he had great respect, he had decided that it would be a good thing to set fire to the village. "Very good!" said Bagratión in reply to the officer's report, and began deliberately to examine the whole battlefield extended before him. The French had advanced nearest on our right. Below the height on which the Kiev regiment was stationed, in the hollow where the rivulet flowed, the soul-stirring rolling and crackling of musketry was heard, and much farther to the right beyond the dragoons, the officer of the suite pointed out to Bagratión a French column that was outflanking us. To the left the horizon bounded by the adjacent wood. Prince Bagratión ordered two battalions from the center to be sent to reinforce the right flank. The officer of the suite ventured to remark to the prince that if these battalions went away, the guns would remain without support. Prince Bagratión turned to the officer and with his dull eyes looked at him in silence. It seemed to Prince Andrew that the officer's remark was just and that really no answer could be made to it. But at that moment an adjutant galloped up with a message from the commander of the regiment in the hollow and news that immense masses of the French were coming down upon them and that his regiment was in disorder and was retreating upon the Kiev grenadiers. Prince Bagratión bowed his head in sign of assent and approval. He rode off at a walk to the right and sent an adjutant to the dragoons with orders to attack the French. But this adjutant returned half an hour later with the news that the commander of the dragoons had already retreated beyond the dip in the ground, as a heavy fire had been opened on him and he was losing men uselessly, and so had hastened to throw some sharpshooters into the wood.

"Very good!" said Bagratión.

As he was leaving the battery, firing was heard on the left also, and as it was too far to the left flank for him to have time to go there himself, Prince Bagratión sent Zherkóv to tell the general in command (the one who had paraded his regiment before Kutúzov at Braunau) that he must retreat as quickly as possible behind the hollow in the rear, as the right flank would probably not be able to withstand the enemy's attack very long. About Túshin and the battalion that had been in support of his battery all was forgotten. Prince Andrew listened attentively to Bagratión's colloquies with the commanding officers and the orders he gave them and, to his surprise, found that no orders were really given, but that Prince Bagratión tried to make it appear that everything done by necessity, by accident, or by the will of subordinate commanders was done, if not by his direct command, at least in accord with his intentions. Prince Andrew noticed, however, that though what happened was due to chance and was independent of the commander's will, owing to the tact Bagratión showed, his presence was very valuable. Officers who approached him with disturbed countenances became calm; soldiers and officers greeted him gaily, grew more cheerful in his presence, and were evidently anxious to display their courage before him.

CHAPTER XVIII

Prince Bagratión, having reached the highest point of our right flank, began riding downhill to where the roll of musketry was heard but where on account of the smoke nothing could be seen. The nearer they got to the hollow the less they could see but the more they felt the nearness of the actual battlefield. They began to meet wounded men. One with a bleeding head and no cap was being dragged along by two soldiers who supported him under the arms. There was a gurgle in his throat and he was spitting blood. A bullet had evidently hit him in the throat or mouth. Another was walking sturdily by himself but without his musket, groaning aloud and swinging his arm which had just been hurt, while blood from it was streaming over his greatcoat as from a bottle. He had that moment been wounded and his face showed fear rather than suffering. Crossing a road they descended a steep incline and saw several men lying on the ground; they also met a crowd of soldiers some of whom were unwounded. The soldiers were ascending the hill breathing heavily, and despite the general's presence were talking loudly and gesticulating. In front of them rows of gray cloaks were already visible through the smoke, and an officer catching sight of Bagratiónrushed shouting after the crowd of retreating soldiers, ordering them back. Bagratión rode up to the ranks along which shots crackled now here and now there, drowning the sound of voices and the shouts of command. The whole air reeked with smoke. The excited faces of the soldiers were blackened with it. Some were using their ramrods, others putting powder on the touchpans or taking charges from their pouches, while others were firing, though who they were firing at could not be seen for the smoke which there was no wind to carry away. A pleasant humming and whistling of bullets were often heard. "What is this?" thought Prince

Andrew approaching the crowd of soldiers. "It can't be an attack, for they are not moving; it can't be a square—for they are not drawn up for that."

The commander of the regiment, a thin, feeble-looking old man with a pleasant smile—his eyelids drooping more than half over his old eyes, giving him a mild expression, rode up to Bagratión and welcomed him as a host welcomes an honored guest. He reported that his regiment had been attacked by French cavalry and that, though the attack had been repulsed, he had lost more than half his men. He said the attack had been repulsed, employing this military term to describe what had occurred to his regiment, but in reality he did not himself know what had happened during that half-hour to the troops entrusted to him, and could not say with certainty whether the attack had been repulsed or his regiment had been broken up. All he knew was that at the commencement of the action balls and shells began flying all over his regiment and hitting men and that afterwards someone had shouted "Cavalry!" and our men had begun firing. They were still firing, not at the cavalry which had disappeared, but at French infantry who had come into the hollow and were firing at our men. Prince Bagratión bowed his head as a sign that this was exactly what he had desired and expected. Turning to his adjutant he ordered him to bring down the two battalions of the Sixth Chasseurs whom they had just passed. Prince Andrew was struck by the changed expression on Prince Bagratión's face at this moment. It expressed the concentrated and happy resolution you see on the face of a man who on a hot day takes a final run before plunging into the water. The dull, sleepy expression was no longer there, nor the affectation of profound thought. The round, steady, hawk's eyes looked before him eagerly and rather disdainfully, not resting on anything although his movements were still slow and measured.

The commander of the regiment turned to Prince Bagratión, entreating him to go back as it was too dangerous to remain where they were. "Please, your excellency, for God's sake!" he kept saying, glancing for support at an officer of the suite who turned away from him. "There, you see!" and he drew attention to the bullets whistling, singing, and hissing continually around them. He spoke in the tone of entreaty and reproach that a carpenter uses to a gentleman who has picked up an ax: "We are used to it, but you, sir, will blister your hands." He spoke as if those bullets could not kill him, and his half-closed eyes gave still more persuasiveness to his words. The staff officer joined in the colonel's appeals, but Bagratión did not reply; he only gave an order to cease firing and re-form, so as to give room for the two approaching battalions. While he was speaking, the curtain of smoke that had concealed the hollow, driven by a rising wind, began to move from right to left as if drawn by an invisible hand, and the hill opposite, with the French moving about on it, opened out before them. All eyes fastened involuntarily on this French column advancing against them and winding down over the uneven ground. One could already see the soldiers' shaggy caps, distinguish the officers from the men, and see the standard flapping against its staff.

"They march splendidly," remarked someone in Bagratión's suite.

The head of the column had already descended into the hollow. The clash would take place on this side of it...

The remains of our regiment which had been in action rapidly formed up and moved to the right; from behind it, dispersing the laggards, came two battalions of the Sixth Chasseurs in fine order. Before they had reached Bagratión, the weighty tread of the mass of men marching in step could be heard. On their left flank, nearest to Bagratión, marched a company commander, a fine round-faced man, with a stupid and happy expression—the same man who had rushed out of the wattle shed. At that moment he was clearly thinking of nothing but how dashing a fellow he would appear as he passed the commander.

With the self-satisfaction of a man on parade, he stepped lightly with his muscular legs as if sailing along, stretching himself to his full height without the smallest effort, his ease contrasting with the heavy tread of the soldiers who were keeping step with him. He carried close to his leg a narrow unsheathed sword (small, curved, and not like a real weapon) and looked now at the superior officers and now back at the men without losing step, his whole powerful body turning flexibly. It was as if all the powers of his soul were concentrated on passing the commander in the best possible manner, and feeling that he was doing it well he was happy. "Left... left... left..." he seemed to repeat to himself at each alternate step; and in time to this, with stern but varied faces, the wall of soldiers burdened with knapsacks and muskets marched in step, and each one of these hundreds of soldiers seemed to be repeating to himself at each alternate step, "Left... left... left..." A fat major skirted a bush, puffing and falling out of step; a soldier who had fallen behind, his face showing alarm at his defection, ran at a trot, panting to catch up with his company. A cannon ball, cleaving the air, flew over the heads of Bagratión and his suite, and fell into the column to the measure of *"Left... left!"* "Close up!" came the company commander's voice in jaunty tones. The soldiers passed in a semicircle round something where the ball had fallen, and an old trooper on the flank, a noncommissioned officer who had stopped beside the dead men, ran to catch up his line and, falling into step with a hop, looked back angrily, and through the ominous silence and the regular tramp of feet beating the ground in unison, one seemed to hear *left... left... left.*

"Well done, lads!" said Prince Bagratión.

"Glad to do our best, your ex'len-lency!" came a confused shout from the ranks. A morose soldier marching on the left turned his eyes on Bagratión as he shouted, with an expression that seemed to say: "We know that ourselves!" Another, without looking round, as though fearing to relax, shouted with his mouth wide open and passed on.

The order was given to halt and down knapsacks.

Bagratión rode round the ranks that had marched past him and dismounted. He gave the reins to a Cossack, took off and handed over his felt coat, stretched his legs, and set his cap straight. The head of the French column, with its officers leading, appeared from below the hill.

"Forward, with God!" said Bagratión, in a resolute, sonorous voice, turning for a moment to the front line, and slightly swinging his arms, he went forward uneasily over the rough field with the awkward gait of a cavalryman. Prince Andrew felt that an invisible power was leading him forward, and experienced great happiness.

The French were already near. Prince Andrew, walking beside Bagratión, could clearly distinguish their bandoliers, red epaulets, and even their faces. (He distinctly saw an old French officer who, with gaitered legs and turned-out toes, climbed the hill with difficulty.) Prince Bagratión gave no further orders and silently continued to walk on in front of the ranks. Suddenly one shot after another rang out from the French, smoke appeared all along their uneven ranks, and musket shots sounded. Several of our men fell, among them the round-faced officer who had marched so gaily and complacently. But at the moment the first report was heard, Bagratión looked round and shouted, "Hurrah!"

"Hurrah—ah!—ah!" rang a long-drawn shout from our ranks, and passing Bagratión and racing one another they rushed in an irregular but joyous and eager crowd down the hill at their disordered foe.

CHAPTER XIX

The attack of the Sixth Chasseurs secured the retreat of our right flank. In the centerTúshin's forgotten battery, which had managed to set fire to the Schön Grabern village, delayed the French advance. The French were putting out the fire which the wind was spreading, and thus gave us time to retreat. The retirement of the center to the other side of the dip in the ground at the rear was hurried and noisy, but the different companies did not get mixed. But our left—which consisted of the Azóv and Podólsk infantry and the Pávlograd hussars—was simultaneously attacked and outflanked by superior French forces under Lannes and was thrown into confusion. Bagratión had sent Zherkóv to the general commanding that left flank with orders to retreat immediately.

Zherkóv, not removing his hand from his cap, turned his horse about and galloped off. But no sooner had he left Bagratión than his courage failed him. He was seized by panic and could not go where it was dangerous.

Having reached the left flank, instead of going to the front where the firing was, he began to look for the general and his staff where they could not possibly be, and so did not deliver the order.

The command of the left flank belonged by seniority to the commander of the regiment Kutúzov had reviewed at Braunau and in which Dólokhov was serving as a private. But the command of the extreme left flank had been assigned to the commander of the Pávlograd regiment in which Rostóv was serving, and a misunderstanding arose. The two commanders were much exasperated with one another and, long after the action had begun on the right flank and the French were already advancing, were engaged in discussion with the sole object of offending one another. But the regiments, both cavalry and infantry, were by no means ready for the impending action. From privates to general they were not expecting a battle and were engaged in peaceful occupations, the cavalry feeding the horses and the infantry collecting wood.

"He higher iss dan I in rank," said the German colonel of the hussars, flushing and addressing an adjutant who had ridden up, "so let him do what he vill, but I cannot sacrifice my hussars... Bugler, sountze retreat!"

But haste was becoming imperative. Cannon and musketry, mingling together, thundered on the right and in the center, while the capotes of Lannes' sharpshooters were already seen crossing the milldam and forming up within twice the range of a musket shot. The general in command of the infantry went toward his horse with jerky steps, and having mounted drew himself up very straight and tall and rode to the Pávlograd commander. The commanders met with polite bows but with secret malevolence in their hearts.

"Once again, Colonel," said the general, "I can't leave half my men in the wood. I *beg* of you, I *beg* of you," he repeated, "to occupy the *position* and prepare for an attack."

"I *peg* of you yourself not to mix in vot is not your business!" suddenly replied the irate colonel. "If you vere in the cavalry..."

"I am not in the cavalry, Colonel, but I am a Russian general and if you are not aware of the fact..."

"Quite avare, your excellency," suddenly shouted the colonel, touching his horse and turning purple in the face. "Vill you be so goot to come to ze front and see datzis position iss no goot? I don't vish to destroy my men for your pleasure!"

"You forget yourself, Colonel. I am not considering my own pleasure and I won't allow it to be said!"

Taking the colonel's outburst as a challenge to his courage, the general expanded his chest and rode, frowning, beside him to the front line, as if their differences would be settled there amongst the bullets. They reached the front, several bullets sped over them, and they halted in silence. There was nothing fresh to be seen from the line, for from where they had been before it had been evident that it was impossible for cavalry to act among the bushes and broken ground, as well as that the French were outflanking our left. The general and colonel looked sternly and significantly at one another like two fighting cocks preparing for battle, each vainly trying to detect signs of cowardice in the other. Both passed the examination successfully. As there was nothing to be said, and neither wished to give occasion for it to be alleged that he had been the first to leave the range of fire, they would have remained there for a long time testing each other's courage had it not been that just then they heard the rattle of musketry and a muffled shout almost behind them in the wood. The French had attacked the men collecting wood in the copse. It was no longer possible for the hussars to retreat with the infantry. They were cut off from the line of retreat on the left by the French. However inconvenient the position, it was now necessary to attack in order to cut a way through for themselves.

The squadron in which Rostóv was serving had scarcely time to mount before it was halted facing the enemy. Again, as at the Enns bridge, there was nothing between the squadron and the enemy, and again that terrible dividing line of uncertainty and fear—resembling the line separating the living from the dead—lay between them. All were conscious of this unseen line, and the question whether they would cross it or not, and how they would cross it, agitated them all.

The colonel rode to the front, angrily gave some reply to questions put to him by the officers, and, like a man desperately insisting on having his own way, gave an order. No one said anything definite, but the rumor of an attack spread through the squadron. The command to form up rang out and the sabers whizzed as they were drawn from their scabbards. Still no one moved. The troops of the left flank, infantry and hussars alike, felt that the commander did not himself know what to do, and this irresolution communicated itself to the men.

"If only they would be quick!" thought Rostóv, feeling that at last the time had come to experience the joy of an attack of which he had so often heard from his fellow hussars.

"Fo'ward, with God, lads!" rang out Denísov's voice. "At a twotfo'ward!"

The horses' croups began to sway in the front line. Rook pulled at the reins and started of his own accord.

Before him, on the right, Rostóv saw the front lines of his hussars and still farther ahead a dark line which he could not see distinctly but took to be the enemy. Shots could be heard, but some way off.

"Faster!" came the word of command, and Rostóv felt Rook's flanks drooping as he broke into a gallop.

Rostóv anticipated his horse's movements and became more and more elated. He had noticed a solitary tree ahead of him. This tree had been in the middle of the line that had seemed so terrible—and now he had crossed that line and not only was there nothing terrible, but everything was becoming more and more happy and animated. "Oh, how I will slash at him!" thought Rostóv, gripping the hilt of his saber.

"Hur-a-a-a-ah!" came a roar of voices. "Let anyone come my way now," thought Rostóv driving his spurs into Rook and letting him go at a full gallop so that he outstripped the others. Ahead, the enemy was already visible. Suddenly something like a birch broom seemed to sweep over the squadron. Rostóv raised his saber, ready to strike, but at that instant the trooper Nikítenko, who was galloping ahead, shot away from him, and Rostóv felt as in a dream that he continued to be carried forward with unnatural speed but yet stayed on the same spot. From behind him Bondarchúk, an hussar he knew, jolted against him and looked angrily at him. Bondarchúk's horse swerved and galloped past.

"How is it I am not moving? I have fallen, I am killed!" Rostóv asked and answered at the same instant. He was alone in the middle of a field. Instead of the moving horses and hussars' backs, he saw nothing before him but the motionless earth and the stubble around him. There was warm blood under his arm. "No, I am wounded and the horse is killed." Rook tried to rise on his forelegs but fell back, pinning his rider's leg. Blood was flowing from his head; he struggled but could not rise. Rostóv also tried to rise but fell back, his sabretache having become entangled in the saddle. Where our men were, and where the French, he did not know. There was no one near.

Having disentangled his leg, he rose. "Where, on which side, was now the line that had so sharply divided the two armies?" he asked himself and could not answer. "Can something bad have happened to me?" he wondered as he got up: and at that moment he felt that something superfluous was hanging on his benumbed left arm. The wrist felt as if it were not his. He examined his hand carefully, vainly trying to find blood on it. "Ah, here are people coming," he thought joyfully, seeing some men running toward him. "They will help me!" In front came a man wearing a strange shako and a blue cloak, swarthy, sunburned, and with a hooked nose. Then came two more, and many more running behind. One of them said something strange, not in Russian. In among the hindmost of these men wearing similar shakos was a Russian hussar. He was being held by the arms and his horse was being led behind him.

"It must be one of ours, a prisoner. Yes. Can it be that they will take me too? Who are these men?" thought Rostóv, scarcely believing his eyes. "Can they be French?" He looked at the approaching Frenchmen, and though but a moment before he had been galloping to get at them and hack them to pieces, their proximity now seemed so awful that he could not believe his eyes. "Who are they? Why are they running? Can they be coming at me? And why? To kill me? *Me* whom everyone is so fond of?" He remembered his mother's love for him, and his family's, and his friends', and the enemy's intention to kill him seemed impossible. "But perhaps they may do it!" For more than ten seconds he stood not moving from the spot or realizing the situation. The foremost Frenchman, the one with the hooked nose, was already so close that the expression of his face could be seen. And the excited, alien face of that man, his bayonet hanging down, holding his breath, and running so lightly, frightened Rostóv. He seized his pistol and, instead of firing it, flung it at the Frenchman and ran with all his might toward the bushes. He did not now run with the feeling of doubt and conflict with which he had trodden the Enns bridge, but with the feeling of a hare fleeing from the hounds. One single sentiment, that of fear for his young and happy life, possessed his whole being. Rapidly leaping the furrows, he fled across the field with the impetuosity he used to show at catchplay, now and then turning his good-natured, pale, young face to look back. A shudder of terror went through him: "No, better not look," he thought, but having reached the bushes he glanced round once more. The French had fallen behind, and just as he looked round the first man changed his run to a walk and, turning, shouted something loudly to a comrade farther back. Rostóv paused. "No, there's some mistake," thought he. "They can't have wanted to kill me." But at the same time, his left arm felt as heavy as if a seventy-pound weight were tied to it. He could run no more. The Frenchman also stopped and took aim. Rostóv closed his eyes and stooped down. One bullet and then another whistled past him. He mustered his last remaining strength, took hold of his left hand with his right, and reached the bushes. Behind these were some Russian sharpshooters.

CHAPTER XX

The infantry regiments that had been caught unawares in the outskirts of the wood ran out of it, the different companies getting mixed, and retreated as a disorderly crowd. One soldier, in his fear, uttered the senseless cry, "Cut off!" that is so terrible in battle, and that word infected the whole crowd with a feeling of panic.

"Surrounded! Cut off? We're lost!" shouted the fugitives.

The moment he heard the firing and the cry from behind, the general realized that something dreadful had happened to his regiment, and the thought that he, an exemplary officer of many years' service who had never been to blame, might be held responsible at headquarters for negligence or inefficiency so staggered him that, forgetting the recalcitrant cavalry colonel, his own dignity as a general, and above all quite forgetting the danger and all regard for self-preservation, he clutched the crupper of his saddle and, spurring his horse, galloped to the regiment under a hail of bullets which fell around, but fortunately missed him. His one desire was to know what was happening and at any cost correct, or remedy, the mistake if he had made one, so that he, an exemplary officer of twenty-two years' service, who had never been censured, should not be held to blame.

Having galloped safely through the French, he reached a field behind the copse across which our men, regardless of orders, were running and descending the valley. That moment of moral hesitation which decides the fate of battles had arrived. Would this disorderly crowd of soldiers attend to the voice of their commander, or would they, disregarding him, continue their flight? Despite his desperate shouts that used to seem so terrible to the soldiers, despite his furious purple countenance distorted out of all likeness to his former self, and the flourishing of his saber, the soldiers all continued to run, talking, firing into the air, and disobeying orders. The moral hesitation which decided the fate of battles was evidently culminating in a panic.

The general had a fit of coughing as a result of shouting and of the powder smoke and stopped in despair. Everything seemed lost. But at that moment the French who were attacking, suddenly and without any apparent reason, ran back and disappeared from the outskirts, and Russian sharpshooters showed themselves in the copse. It was Timókhin's company, which alone had maintained its order in the wood and, having lain in ambush in a ditch, now attacked the French unexpectedly. Timókhin, armed only with a sword, had rushed at the enemy with such a desperate cry and such mad, drunken determination that, taken by surprise, the French had thrown down their muskets and run. Dólokhov, running beside Timókhin, killed a Frenchman at close quarters and was the first to seize the surrendering French officer by his collar. Our fugitives returned, the battalions re-formed, and the French who had nearly cut our left flank in half were for the moment repulsed. Our reserve units were able to join up, and the fight was at an end. The regimental commander and Major Ekonómov had stopped beside a bridge, letting the retreating companies pass by them, when a soldier came up and took hold of the commander's stirrup, almost leaning against him. The man was wearing a bluish coat of broadcloth, he had no knapsack or cap, his head was bandaged, and over his shoulder a French munition pouch was slung. He had an officer's sword in his hand. The soldier was pale, his blue eyes looked impudently into the commander's face, and his lips were smiling. Though the commander was occupied in giving instructions to Major Ekonómov, he could not help taking notice of the soldier.

"Your excellency, here are two trophies," said Dólokhov, pointing to the French sword and pouch. "I have taken an officer prisoner. I stopped the company." Dólokhov breathed heavily from weariness and spoke in abrupt sentences. "The whole company can bear witness. I beg you will remember this, your excellency!"

"All right, all right," replied the commander, and turned to Major Ekonómov.

But Dólokhov did not go away; he untied the handkerchief around his head, pulled it off, and showed the blood congealed on his hair.

"A bayonet wound. I remained at the front. Remember, your excellency!"

Túshin's battery had been forgotten and only at the very end of the action did Prince Bagratión, still hearing the cannonade in the center, send his orderly staff officer, and later Prince Andrew also, to order the battery to retire as quickly as possible. When the supports attached to Túshin's battery had been moved away in the middle of the action by someone's order, the battery had continued firing and was only not captured by the French because the enemy could not surmise that anyone could have the effrontery to continue firing from four quite undefended guns. On the contrary, the energetic action of that battery led the French to suppose that here—in the center—the main Russian forces were concentrated. Twice they had attempted to attack this point, but on each occasion had been driven back by grapeshot from the four isolated guns on the hillock.

Soon after Prince Bagratión had left him, Túshin had succeeded in setting fire to Schön Grabern.

"Look at them scurrying! It's burning! Just see the smoke! Fine! Grand! Look at the smoke, the smoke!" exclaimed the artillerymen, brightening up.

All the guns, without waiting for orders, were being fired in the direction of the conflagration. As if urging each other on, the soldiers cried at each shot: "Fine! That's good! Look at it... Grand!" The fire, fanned by the breeze, was rapidly spreading. The French columns that had advanced beyond the village went back; but as though in revenge for this failure, the enemy placed ten guns to the right of the village and began firing them at Túshin's battery.

In their childlike glee, aroused by the fire and their luck in successfully cannonading the French, our artillerymen only noticed this battery when two balls, and then four more, fell among our guns, one knocking over two horses and another tearing off a munition-wagon driver's leg. Their spirits once roused were, however, not diminished, but only changed character. The horses were replaced by others from a reserve gun carriage, the wounded were carried away, and the four guns were turned against the ten-gun battery. Túshin's companion officer had been killed at the beginning of the engagement and within an hour seventeen of the forty men of the guns' crews had been disabled, but the artillerymen were still as merry and lively as ever. Twice they noticed the French appearing below them, and then they fired grapeshot at them.

Little Túshin, moving feebly and awkwardly, kept telling his orderly to "refill my pipe for that one!" and then, scattering sparks from it, ran forward shading his eyes with his small hand to look at the French.

"Smack at 'em, lads!" he kept saying, seizing the guns by the wheels and working the screws himself.

Amid the smoke, deafened by the incessant reports which always made him jump, Túshin not taking his pipe from his mouth ran from gun to gun, now aiming, now counting the charges, now giving orders about replacing dead or wounded horses and harnessing fresh ones, and shouting in his feeble voice, so high pitched and irresolute. His face grew more and more animated. Only when a man was killed or wounded did he frown and turn away from the sight, shouting angrily at the men who, as is always the case, hesitated about lifting the injured or dead. The soldiers, for the most part handsome fellows and, as is always the case in an artillery company, a head and shoulders taller and twice as broad as their officer—all looked at their commander like children in an embarrassing situation, and the expression on his face was invariably reflected on theirs.

Owing to the terrible uproar and the necessity for concentration and activity, Túshin did not experience the slightest unpleasant sense of fear, and the thought that he might be killed or badly wounded never occurred to him. On the contrary, he became more and more elated. It seemed to him that it was a very long time ago, almost a day, since he had first seen the enemy and fired the first shot, and that the corner of the field he stood on was well-known and familiar ground. Though he thought of everything, considered everything, and did everything the best of officers could do in his position, he was in a state akin to feverish delirium or drunkenness.

From the deafening sounds of his own guns around him, the whistle and thud of the enemy's cannon balls, from the flushed and perspiring faces of the crew bustling round the guns, from the sight of the blood of men and horses, from the little puffs of smoke on the enemy's side (always followed by a ball flying past and striking the earth, a man, a gun, a horse), from the sight of all these things a fantastic world of his own had taken possession of his brain and at that moment afforded him pleasure. The enemy's guns were in his fancy not guns but pipes from which occasional puffs were blown by an invisible smoker.

"There... he's puffing again," muttered Túshin to himself, as a small cloud rose from the hill and was borne in a streak to the left by the wind.

"Now look out for the ball... we'll throw it back."

"What do you want, your honor?" asked an artilleryman, standing close by, who heard him muttering.

"Nothing... only a shell..." he answered.

"Come along, our Matvévna!" he said to himself. "Matvévna" * was the name his fancy gave to the farthest gun of the battery, which was large and of an old pattern. The French swarming round their guns seemed to him like ants. In that world, the handsome drunkard Number One of the second gun's crew was "uncle"; Túshin looked at him more often than at anyone else and took delight in his every movement. The sound of musketry at the foot of the hill, now diminishing, now increasing, seemed like someone's breathing. He listened intently to the ebb and flow of these sounds.

* Daughter of Matthew.

"Ah! Breathing again, breathing!" he muttered to himself.

He imagined himself as an enormously tall, powerful man who was throwing cannon balls at the French with both hands.

"Now then, Matvévna, dear old lady, don't let me down!" he was saying as he moved from the gun, when a strange, unfamiliar voice called above his head: "Captain Túshin! Captain!"

Túshin turned round in dismay. It was the staff officer who had turned him out of the booth at Grunth. He was shouting in a gasping voice:

"Are you mad? You have twice been ordered to retreat, and you..."

"Why are they down on me?" thought Túshin, looking in alarm at his superior.

"I... don't..." he muttered, holding up two fingers to his cap. "I..."

But the staff officer did not finish what he wanted to say. A cannon ball, flying close to him, caused him to duck and bend over his horse. He paused, and just as he was about to say something more, another ball stopped him. He turned his horse and galloped off.

"Retire! All to retire!" he shouted from a distance.

The soldiers laughed. A moment later, an adjutant arrived with the same order.

It was Prince Andrew. The first thing he saw on riding up to the space where Túshin's guns were stationed was an unharnessed horse with a broken leg, that lay screaming piteously beside the harnessed horses. Blood was gushing from its leg as from a spring. Among the limbers lay several dead men. One ball after another passed over as he approached and he felt a nervous shudder run down his spine. But the mere thought of being afraid roused him again. "I cannot be afraid," thought he, and dismounted slowly among the guns. He delivered the order and did not leave the battery. He decided to have the guns removed from their positions and withdrawn in his presence. Together with Túshin, stepping across the bodies and under a terrible fire from the French, he attended to the removal of the guns.

"A staff officer was here a minute ago, but skipped off," said an artilleryman to Prince Andrew. "Not like your honor!"

Prince Andrew said nothing to Túshin. They were both so busy as to seem not to notice one another. When having limbered up the only two cannon that remained uninjured out of the four, they began moving down the hill (one shattered gun and one unicorn were left behind), Prince Andrew rode up to Túshin.

"Well, till we meet again..." he said, holding out his hand to Túshin.

"Good-by, my dear fellow," said Túshin. "Dear soul! Good-by, my dear fellow!" and for some unknown reason tears suddenly filled his eyes.

CHAPTER XXI

The wind had fallen and black clouds, merging with the powder smoke, hung low over the field of battle on the horizon. It was growing dark and the glow of two conflagrations was the more conspicuous. The cannonade was dying down, but the rattle of musketry behind and on the right sounded oftener and nearer. As soon as Túshin with his guns, continually driving round or coming upon wounded men, was out of range of fire and had descended into the dip, he was met by some of the staff, among them the staff officer and Zherkóv, who had been twice sent to Túshin's battery but had never reached it. Interrupting one another, they all gave, and transmitted, orders as to how to proceed, reprimanding and reproaching him. Túshin gave no orders, and, silently—fearing to speak because at every word he felt ready to weep without knowing why—rode behind on his artillery nag. Though the orders were to abandon the wounded, many of them dragged themselves after troops and begged for seats on the gun carriages. The jaunty infantry officer who just before the battle had rushed out of Túshin's wattle shed was laid, with a bullet in his stomach, on "Matvévna's" carriage. At the foot of the hill, a pale hussar cadet, supporting one hand with the other, came up to Túshin and asked for a seat.

"Captain, for God's sake! I've hurt my arm," he said timidly. "For God's sake... I can't walk. For God's sake!"

It was plain that this cadet had already repeatedly asked for a lift and been refused. He asked in a hesitating, piteous voice.

"Tell them to give me a seat, for God's sake!"

"Give him a seat," said Túshin. "Lay a cloak for him to sit on, lad," he said, addressing his favorite soldier. "And where is the wounded officer?"

"He has been set down. He died," replied someone.

"Help him up. Sit down, dear fellow, sit down! Spread out the cloak, Antónov."

The cadet was Rostóv. With one hand he supported the other; he was pale and his jaw trembled, shivering feverishly. He was placed on "Matvévna," the gun from which they had removed the dead officer. The cloak they spread under him was wet with blood which stained his breeches and arm.

"What, are you wounded, my lad?" said Túshin, approaching the gun on which Rostóv sat.

"No, it's a sprain."

"Then what is this blood on the gun carriage?" inquired Túshin.

"It was the officer, your honor, stained it," answered the artilleryman, wiping away the blood with his coat sleeve, as if apologizing for the state of his gun.

It was all that they could do to get the guns up the rise aided by the infantry, and having reached the village of Gruntersdorf they halted. It had grown so dark that one could not distinguish the uniforms ten paces off, and the firing had begun to subside. Suddenly, near by on the right, shouting and firing were again heard. Flashes of shot gleamed in the darkness. This was the last French attack and was met by soldiers who had sheltered in the village houses. They all rushed out of the village again, but Túshin's guns could not move, and the artillerymen, Túshin, and the cadet exchanged silent glances as they awaited their fate. The firing died down and soldiers, talking eagerly, streamed out of a side street.

"Not hurt, Petróv?" asked one.

"We've given it 'em hot, mate! They won't make another push now," said another.

"You couldn't see a thing. How they shot at their own fellows! Nothing could be seen. Pitch-dark, brother! Isn't there something to drink?"

The French had been repulsed for the last time. And again and again in the complete darkness Túshin's guns moved forward, surrounded by the humming infantry as by a frame.

In the darkness, it seemed as though a gloomy unseen river was flowing always in one direction, humming with whispers and talk and the sound of hoofs and wheels. Amid the general rumble, the groans and voices of the wounded were more distinctly heard than any other sound in the darkness of the night. The gloom that enveloped the army was filled with their groans, which seemed to melt into one with the darkness of the night. After a while the moving mass became agitated, someone rode past on a white horse followed by his suite, and said something in passing: "What did he say? Where to, now? Halt, is it? Did he thank us?" came eager questions from all sides. The whole moving mass began pressing closer together and a report spread that they were ordered to halt: evidently those in front had halted. All remained where they were in the middle of the muddy road.

Fires were lighted and the talk became more audible. Captain Túshin, having given orders to his company, sent a soldier to find a dressing station or a doctor for the cadet, and sat down by a bonfire the soldiers had kindled on the road. Rostóv, too, dragged himself to the fire. From pain, cold, and damp, a feverish shivering shook his whole body. Drowsiness was irresistibly mastering him, but he kept awake by an excruciating pain in his arm, for which he could find no satisfactory position. He kept closing his eyes and then again looking at the fire, which seemed to him dazzlingly red, and at the feeble, round-shouldered figure of Túshin who was sitting cross-legged like a Turk beside him. Túshin's large, kind, intelligent eyes were fixed with sympathy and commiseration on Rostóv, who saw that Túshin with his whole heart wished to help him but could not.

From all sides were heard the footsteps and talk of the infantry, who were walking, driving past, and settling down all around. The sound of voices, the tramping feet, the horses' hoofs moving in mud, the crackling of wood fires near and afar, merged into one tremulous rumble.

It was no longer, as before, a dark, unseen river flowing through the gloom, but a dark sea swelling and gradually subsiding after a storm. Rostóv looked at and listened listlessly to what passed before and around him. An infantryman came to the fire, squatted on his heels, held his hands to the blaze, and turned away his face.

"You don't mind your honor?" he asked Túshin. "I've lost my company, your honor. I don't know where... such bad luck!"

With the soldier, an infantry officer with a bandaged cheek came up to the bonfire, and addressing Túshin asked him to have the guns moved a trifle to let a wagon go past. After he had gone, two soldiers rushed to the campfire. They were quarreling and fighting desperately, each trying to snatch from the other a boot they were both holding on to.

"You picked it up?... I dare say! You're very smart!" one of them shouted hoarsely.

Then a thin, pale soldier, his neck bandaged with a bloodstained leg band, came up and in angry tones asked the artillerymen for water.

"Must one die like a dog?" said he.

Túshin told them to give the man some water. Then a cheerful soldier ran up, begging a little fire for the infantry.

"A nice little hot torch for the infantry! Good luck to you, fellow countrymen. Thanks for the fire—we'll return it with interest," said he, carrying away into the darkness a glowing stick.

Next came four soldiers, carrying something heavy on a cloak, and passed by the fire. One of them stumbled.

"Who the devil has put the logs on the road?" snarled he.

"He's dead—why carry him?" said another.

"Shut up!"

And they disappeared into the darkness with their load.

"Still aching?" Túshin asked Rostóv in a whisper.

"Yes."

"Your honor, you're wanted by the general. He is in the hut here," said a gunner, coming up to Túshin.

"Coming, friend."

Túshin rose and, buttoning his greatcoat and pulling it straight, walked away from the fire.

Not far from the artillery campfire, in a hut that had been prepared for him, Prince Bagratión sat at dinner, talking with some commanding officers who had gathered at his quarters. The little old man with the half-closed eyes was there greedily gnawing a mutton bone, and the general who had served blamelessly for twenty-two years, flushed by a glass of vodka and the dinner; and the staff officer with the signet ring, and Zherkóv, uneasily glancing at them all, and Prince Andrew, pale, with compressed lips and feverishly glittering eyes.

In a corner of the hut stood a standard captured from the French, and the accountant with the naïve face was feeling its texture, shaking his head in perplexity—perhaps because the banner really interested him, perhaps because it was hard for him, hungry as he was, to look on at a dinner where there was no place for him. In the next hut there was a French colonel who had been taken prisoner by our dragoons. Our officers were flocking in to look at him. Prince Bagratión was thanking the individual commanders and inquiring into details of the action and our losses. The general whose regiment had been inspected at Braunau was informing the prince that as soon as the action began he had withdrawn from the wood, mustered the men who were woodcutting, and, allowing the French to pass him, had made a bayonet charge with two battalions and had broken up the French troops.

"When I saw, your excellency, that their first battalion was disorganized, I stopped in the road and thought: 'I'll let them come on and will meet them with the fire of the whole battalion'—and that's what I did."

The general had so wished to do this and was so sorry he had not managed to do it that it seemed to him as if it had really happened. Perhaps it might really have been so? Could one possibly make out amid all that confusion what did or did not happen?

"By the way, your excellency, I should inform you," he continued—remembering Dólokhov's conversation with Kutúzov and his last interview with the gentleman-ranker—"that Private Dólokhov, who was reduced to the ranks, took a French officer prisoner in my presence and particularly distinguished himself."

"I saw the Pávlograd hussars attack there, your excellency," chimed in Zherkóv, looking uneasily around. He had not seen the hussars all that day, but had heard about them from an infantry officer. "They broke up two squares, your excellency."

Several of those present smiled at Zherkóv's words, expecting one of his usual jokes, but noticing that what he was saying redounded to the glory of our arms and of the day's work, they assumed a serious expression, though many of them knew that what he was saying was a lie devoid of any foundation. Prince Bagratión turned to the old colonel:

"Gentlemen, I thank you all; all arms have behaved heroically: infantry, cavalry, and artillery. How was it that two guns were abandoned in the center?" he inquired, searching with his eyes for someone. (Prince Bagratión did not ask about the guns on the left flank; he knew that all the guns there had been abandoned at the very beginning of the action.) "I think I sent you?" he added, turning to the staff officer on duty.

"One was damaged," answered the staff officer, "and the other I can't understand. I was there all the time giving orders and had only just left.... It is true that it was hot there," he added, modestly.

Someone mentioned that Captain Túshin was bivouacking close to the village and had already been sent for.

"Oh, but you were there?" said Prince Bagratión, addressing Prince Andrew.

"Of course, we only just missed one another," said the staff officer, with a smile to Bolkónski.

"I had not the pleasure of seeing you," said Prince Andrew, coldly and abruptly.

All were silent. Túshin appeared at the threshold and made his way timidly from behind the backs of the generals. As he stepped past the generals in the crowded hut, feeling embarrassed as he always was by the sight of his superiors, he did not notice the staff of the banner and stumbled over it. Several of those present laughed.

"How was it a gun was abandoned?" asked Bagratión, frowning, not so much at the captain as at those who were laughing, among whom Zherkóv laughed loudest.

Only now, when he was confronted by the stern authorities, did his guilt and the disgrace of having lost two guns and yet remaining alive present themselves to Túshin in all their horror. He had been so excited that he had not thought about it until that moment. The officers' laughter confused him still more. He stood before Bagratión with his lower jaw trembling and was hardly able to mutter: "I don't know... your excellency... I had no men... your excellency."

"You might have taken some from the covering troops."

Túshin did not say that there were no covering troops, though that was perfectly true. He was afraid of getting some other officer into trouble, and silently fixed his eyes on Bagratión as a schoolboy who has blundered looks at an examiner.

The silence lasted some time. Prince Bagratión, apparently not wishing to be severe, found nothing to say; the others did not venture to intervene. Prince Andrew looked at Túshin from under his brows and his fingers twitched nervously.

"Your excellency!" Prince Andrew broke the silence with his abrupt voice, "you were pleased to send me to Captain Túshin's battery. I went there and found two thirds of the men and horses knocked out, two guns smashed, and no supports at all."

Prince Bagratión and Túshin looked with equal intentness at Bolkónski, who spoke with suppressed agitation.

"And, if your excellency will allow me to express my opinion," he continued, "we owe today's success chiefly to the action of that battery and the heroic endurance of Captain Túshin and his company," and without awaiting a reply, Prince Andrew rose and left the table.

Prince Bagratión looked at Túshin, evidently reluctant to show distrust in Bolkónski's emphatic opinion yet not feeling able fully to credit it, bent his head, and told Túshin that he could go. Prince Andrew went out with him.

"Thank you; you saved me, my dear fellow!" said Túshin.

Prince Andrew gave him a look, but said nothing and went away. He felt sad and depressed. It was all so strange, so unlike what he had hoped.

"Who are they? Why are they here? What do they want? And when will all this end?" thought Rostóv, looking at the changing shadows before him. The pain in his arm became more and more intense. Irresistible drowsiness overpowered him, red rings danced before his eyes, and the impression of those voices and faces and a sense of loneliness merged with the physical pain. It was they, these soldiers—wounded and unwounded—it was they who were crushing, weighing down, and twisting the sinews and scorching the flesh of his sprained arm and shoulder. To rid himself of them he closed his eyes.

For a moment he dozed, but in that short interval innumerable things appeared to him in a dream: his mother and her large white hand, Sónya's thin little shoulders, Natásha's eyes and laughter, Denísov with his voice and mustache, and Telyánin and all that affair with Telyánin and Bogdánich. That affair was the same thing as this soldier with the harsh voice, and it was that affair and this soldier that were so agonizingly, incessantly pulling and pressing his arm and always dragging it in one direction. He tried to get away from them, but they would not for an instant let his shoulder move a hair's breadth. It would not ache—it would be well—if only they did not pull it, but it was impossible to get rid of them.

He opened his eyes and looked up. The black canopy of night hung less than a yard above the glow of the charcoal. Flakes of falling snow were fluttering in that light. Túshin had not returned, the doctor had not come. He was alone now, except for a soldier who was sitting naked at the other side of the fire, warming his thin yellow body.

"Nobody wants me!" thought Rostóv. "There is no one to help me or pity me. Yet I was once at home, strong, happy, and loved." He sighed and, doing so, groaned involuntarily.

"Eh, is anything hurting you?" asked the soldier, shaking his shirt out over the fire, and not waiting for an answer he gave a grunt and added: "What a lot of men have been crippled today—frightful!"

Rostóv did not listen to the soldier. He looked at the snowflakes fluttering above the fire and remembered a Russian winter at his warm, bright home, his fluffy fur coat, his quickly gliding sleigh, his healthy body, and all the affection and care of his family. "And why did I come here?" he wondered.

Next day the French army did not renew their attack, and the remnant of Bagratión's detachment was reunited to Kutúzov's army.